## "I want you to be

Will walked over and stood before her. Carrie tilted her head back.

Her heart pounded its way up into her throat. "Me?"

"Yes." He reached out and took both babies from her, then carried them back to the playpen. Carrie had attached a mobile circus of animals to the railing and Will gave it a spin before he turned back to her.

"Will, how could I be their mother? I'm not..."

"You could marry me."

Dear Reader,

A special new delivery! We are proud to announce the birth of our new bouncing baby series! Each month we'll be bringing you your very own bundle of joy—a cute and delightful romance novel by one of your favorite authors. This series is all about the true labor of love—parenthood and how to survive it! Because, as our heroes and heroines are about to discover, two's company and three (or four...or five) is a family!

First in our series is *Two-Parent Family* by Patricia Knoll. And next month's arrival will be *Three Little Miracles* by Rebecca Winters.

Happy reading!

*The Editors*

# Two-Parent Family
## Patricia Knoll

## *Harlequin Books*

TORONTO • NEW YORK • LONDON
AMSTERDAM • PARIS • SYDNEY • HAMBURG
STOCKHOLM • ATHENS • TOKYO • MILAN
MADRID • WARSAW • BUDAPEST • AUCKLAND

To my two best friends,
Janet Gomez and Marie Rhodes.

ISBN 0-373-03442-3

TWO-PARENT FAMILY

First North American Publication 1997.

Copyright © 1997 by Patricia Knoll.

Printed in U.S.A.

# CHAPTER ONE

"CARRIE, could I speak to you for a minute?"

The quavery voice drew Carrie McCoy around. She had been positioning the wedding guest register at just the perfect angle on its stand and admiring the banks of flowers in the church foyer.

Her face lit up and her caramel-colored eyes brightened when she saw who was at the door. She lifted the hem of her shimmering white gown away from her feet and walked forward excitedly. "Good morning, Marcia. Don't sound so nervous," she said with a laugh. "That's supposed to be my job. Isn't it a beautiful day for a wedding? I guess I'm a traditionalist, but I've always wanted to get married in June. I'm glad the weather is nice. We've worked so hard to make sure everything's perfect. Do you have your dress with you? Do you think your shoes will be comfortable enough? There'll be a lot of standing around, especially if Mrs. Mintnor's solo goes as long as it did last night at rehearsal . . ." Carrie's words stumbled to a halt as she finally focused on her friend's ashen face. "What's wrong?"

"Could you come out here, please?" Marcia Gallatin took a quick look at the masses of roses and gladiolus, her gaze traveling to the open doors leading to the church sanctuary. Blanching even more, she stepped outside.

Gathering her skirts, Carrie hurried after Marcia, who held the door wide for her.

"You don't look well at all. Are you ill?" she asked, searching Marcia's face in concern. Reaching up, she touched her cheek, which felt clammy. "Did you come to say you're too sick to be a bridesmaid? If so, don't worry about it. We can manage just fine—"

"No." Marcia held up her hand, and Carrie saw the small white envelope clutched in her fingers. "Is someone here with you? Your sister, maybe?"

"Ginny and Bret and the kids will be here in a few minutes. Little Nancy's so excited about being flower girl." Carrie made a faint gesture toward the foyer. "And Dad's inside. He's with Reverend Mintnor making sure the sound system is ready. You know how he likes to putter and fuss, especially since we're early, but you know I'm always early for everything, even my own wedding." She knew she was babbling, but she couldn't seem to stop. The sick expression on Marcia's face was sending her into a state of alarm.

"I—I know," the other girl said. "I counted on that." She held out the small envelope even as tears welled in her eyes. "Here."

"Is it Robert?" Carrie asked, fear clutching at her throat. "Is something wrong with him? Has something happened?"

Tears ran from Marcia's eyes, and she began to cry in earnest. "Oh, Carrie. I'm so very sorry to be the one to give you this. I'm so sorry."

Sobbing, she turned and stumbled down the steps. She rushed to her car in the nearly empty parking lot and drove away.

Mouth open in surprise, Carrie stared after her. She had never seen Marcia act this way, not even in high school when such emotional outbursts were common. Something must be horribly wrong. Slipping one of her freshly manicured fingernails under the flap, she ripped open the envelope and jerked out the folded piece of white vellum. Hastily, she smoothed it out so she could read the message.

Her gaze skimmed the words, and she went very still.

*I can't marry you,* Robert Gallatin had written in his very precise hand. *I'm sorry.*

She read it again, then again and again as she tried to absorb the words. Shock tingled through her, and she read it again. Finally, she simply stood and stared at the paper.

A sick wave of horror washed through her as the words began to penetrate.

He couldn't marry her? Why ever not? No explanation. No reason given.

She'd been jilted! The man she loved had cast her off like yesterday's newspaper.

Her hands dropped limply to her sides as she gazed blankly into the distance.

The hydrangea bushes on each side of the wrought-iron banisters stirred in the spring breeze, their heavy blossoms bobbing. Pine trees lining the walkway to the entrance sighed and bent before the wind, but she saw none of it. A gust picked up the hem of her billowing white skirt, sending it and her gossamer veil into a swirl.

Automatically, Carrie reached up one hand to corral her veil and pressed the other one down to keep her skirt from blowing. The crackle of paper caught her attention and she glanced dully at the white envelope. She drew it away and stared at it as thoughts chased each other through her mind.

She had seen him just last night at the rehearsal, and they'd sat side by side at the dinner afterward, receiving congratulatory toasts from their family and friends. He hadn't said anything then about not marrying her. True, he'd hardly said anything at all, but the rehearsal had been hectic, and this wasn't the type of thing he could have said during champagne toasts to their happiness.

Carrie gave a half-hysterical trill of laughter. This was incredible. She couldn't believe it. Her mind couldn't seem to comprehend what it meant, and she realized she was in a state very close to shock.

Her fingers trembled as she folded the paper into its envelope.

It couldn't be true. Robert, gentle, thoughtful Robert wouldn't do such a thing to her. And even if it was true, he would have come to tell her himself, wouldn't he?

She had to speak to him. Whirling, she rushed inside and across the foyer to Reverend Mintnor's office. She breathed her thanks when she saw that the room was empty. Grabbing the phone, she punched out the number for Robert's house— almost her house, too. The phone rang and rang while she clutched the receiver and willed Robert to answer.

She imagined the phone shrilling time after time in the empty house. She pictured the pretty little rooms of the cottage they had decorated together, empty now, waiting for the happy newlyweds to arrive.

When not even the answering machine picked up the call, she knew the note was genuine. Robert always turned off the machine when he didn't want to receive an unwelcome call. Deep in her heart, she hadn't really doubted the note, but now she was sure.

Why? The single-word question echoed over and over in her mind as she moved away from the desk. Without conscious intent, she returned to the front steps of the church.

Again, she stared at the envelope crumpled in her hand. The lump of dismay in her throat grew bigger with each second she contemplated the message. She willed her hand to open. Her fingers peeled away from the crumpled paper in a jerky motion that let the envelope and its hateful contents fall to the step. The wind picked it up and tossed it into the bushes.

Backing away, she looked around. Her father, Hugh, was already inside, as were several other people. Ginny and the other bridesmaids would arrive soon in their raspberry pink dresses and picture hats. The church parking lot would fill up with vehicles belonging to the citizens of Webster, South Carolina, the town where she'd been born and raised. Everyone would be coming to see Carrie McCoy marry Robert Gallatin. She was the youngest daughter of the town's only published novelist who was also the publisher of the local newspaper. She was the sister and sister-in-law of the editors. Robert was the son of a wealthy local family who owned two furniture stores. It was being called the wedding of the year in their small community. Everyone thought Robert was the marital catch of the decade.

At this moment, only Carrie and Marcia knew he didn't want to be caught.

Any second now someone would come looking for her. She would have to tell them. She would have to tell the guests, who would then be sent home. Within minutes the whole town would be whispering that poor little Carrie McCoy had been stood up at the altar.

Humiliation washed over her in a nauseating wave. She clutched at her stomach, crumpling the woven satin ribbons that banded her waist.

She couldn't face them. She absolutely couldn't do it. Her father had always said she had more pride than was probably good for her. It was true, but it was something she couldn't change, and she couldn't stand being pitied.

As if independent of her, Carrie's feet began to move. Across the small porch and down the steps she went. Still in shock, she moved slowly at first, then faster and faster until she was running across the parking lot. She fled into the woods beyond the white clapboard church.

Tree branches plucked at her veil, trying to rip it from her head. She finally unpinned it from her chestnut hair, ruining the careful arrangement of curls. She left the veil where it had snagged on a low-hanging hickory branch. Glancing back, she saw it fluttering in the breeze like the ghostly remnants of her hopes and dreams. A dry sob tore from her throat as she turned and stumbled away.

Within seconds, she had crossed the tiny patch of woods and reached the lightly traveled side road that led home. Turning south, she hitched up her dress and ran.

Pebbles bruised her feet as they poked through the thin soles of the balletlike slippers she had chosen to wear so she wouldn't be taller than Robert.

Robert! Through her mind flashed all their moments together. They had known each other for years because she and Marcia had been good friends. It wasn't until she had finished college, accepted an advertising job in Greenville and moved home that they had begun to date.

She had loved him long before he had loved her, but she'd been so sure they were right for each other. His quiet thoughtfulness had appealed to her. They'd had fun together decorating the little house he had inherited. They had planned to live there and add on once the babies began arriving. Lately, he hadn't wanted to talk about babies, or much of anything else. She had known that something was wrong, but had attributed it to wedding jitters— not cold feet!

Immersed in her thoughts, trying to discern some reason for this calamity, she didn't hear the car until it approached from the curve ahead. It slowed, then brakes squealed. In a rush, the car turned sharply until it was pointing in the same direction she was going. The driver pulled up beside her and stopped so suddenly the vehicle almost stood on its nose.

Dazed, she glanced around to see Will Calhoun looking at her from the front seat of his Mustang convertible. He shoved his sunglasses to the top of his head and called out, ''Carrie, what's wrong? What are you doing out here?''

Carrie said several very unladylike words under her breath. She hadn't seen him in several months, but at this moment, she didn't welcome seeing him at all. His brother was married to her sister, which didn't make them related in any way, but Will thought it gave him the right to comment on her life, her choices, even her chosen career in advertising. Most of the time, she found him insufferable and overbearing.

He was dressed in navy blue dress slacks, light blue shirt and tie. His suit jacket was thrown over the back of the seat beside him. He looked like a man who was on his way to a wedding.

In spite of the mirrored sunglasses he wore, she could see the look of utter amazement on his face.

''Answer me,'' he demanded. ''Where the blazes are you going, Carrie? What are you doing out here all by yourself? The church is in the other direction." He removed his glasses and flipped them onto the dashboard, then raised up in his seat as if to climb out after her.

Carrie took a step back, but she lifted her chin at him. "I know perfectly well where the church is. I just came from there."

"Decide to take a walk before marrying Robert?"

"I decided to take a walk *instead* of marrying Robert," she said fiercely, but honesty compelled her to correct that. "Or, rather, he decided to take a walk."

Will's jaw sagged. "He stood you up?" The words came out in a loud wheeze of disbelief.

Carrie threw her hands out. "Well, announce it to the world, why don't you?"

"I won't need to, everyone will know pretty soon."

"Within minutes," she agreed bitterly. Reluctantly, she explained about the note Robert had sent.

"You mean the coward didn't have the nerve to come and tell you himself?"

"Don't call him that," Carrie insisted, then wondered why she bothered. It's exactly what he was, but she was upset and confused and couldn't seem to sort her thoughts and feelings.

Will jumped out of the car and came around to stand before her. "I can't believe you're defending him."

"Just drop it, please," she said. "I'm not prepared to discuss this right now."

"You need to face up to what he really is," Will said, but he raised his hands, palm out, when she gave him an angry look. "All right. I won't say what I'm thinking."

"For once," she muttered.

Will's eyes narrowed. "Webster's a great little town, but I swear if it was possible to melt gossip and turn it into gold, every citizen here would be a millionaire."

Carrie crossed her arms over her slim waist and glanced up at him. "Don't I know it."

"So instead of facing them, you're running away?"

"That's right," she declared, giving him her most intimidating want-to-make-something-of-it glare.

"Trying to save your pride?"

"Not that it's any of your business, but yes, I am." She tossed her head, and a few more curls tumbled about her ears.

Will gave her look for look, his swift glance taking in her pale cheeks, trembling lips and eyes bright with tears that she refused to let slip out. He nodded. "Good idea. I'll help you."

"What?"

He took her arm, which had gone limp in surprise. "Come on. Get in the car. I'll take you home."

"All—all right," she said, almost stumbling over her gown. Gathering the yards of satin, she waited while he opened the door, shifted a blue file folder to the backseat, then helped her stuff the voluminous skirt into the confined leg space. He slammed the door shut, then dashed around to his side and started the car.

Carrie settled into the plush leather seat as they roared down the road. She was grateful to him for getting her away. Once she reached home, she would hide in her room and decide what to do next. Maybe she was being as much of a coward as Robert was, but at this moment, she didn't care.

When they zipped past the street that led to the white Georgian house in which she had grown up and where her sister and brother-in-law now lived, Carrie whirled to face Will. "I thought you were taking me home."

"I am," he said, his eyes flicking to the rearview mirror. "My home."

"In Charleston!"

"That's right." Casually, he lifted his hand in a wave to Farley Hunkle, the sheriff, who was approaching in his patrol car. Farley's head nearly spun off his neck as he looked around to see Will Calhoun driving Carrie McCoy out of town—away from her own wedding.

"But—but you can't do that," she sputtered. "There are things I need to do."

"What?" His eyes were mocking. "Return wedding gifts?"

"Well, yes. And—"

"Look, Carrie," he broke in impatiently. "Would you rather have it get out that you were stood up at the altar or that you were the one doing the standing up?"

"What do you mean?"

"Right now you and I are the only ones who know, right?"

"And Robert and his sister, Marcia."

"Well, he's not going to tell, because he's done something cowardly and he knows it. Marcia's not going to tell because she's probably as disgusted with him as you are, and she's your friend."

Carrie couldn't deny that. "What's your point?"

"My point is that at this moment in your life would you rather have it seem that Robert found something lacking in you, or you found something lacking in him?"

"Him! Definitely him!"

Will nodded. "That's what I thought. So if you run off to Charleston with me, it will seem like you found something better, right?"

Carrie knew his logic was fuzzy, at the very least, but the idea of being the one doing the dumping, rather than the one being dumped, greatly appealed to her. "I guess that's right."

"You can say that calling off the wedding was by mutual consent. If he's smart, Robert won't argue. He'll look like a fool if he does."

Carrie thought it over for a few seconds, then said slowly, "That might work."

"Of course it will," he answered with supreme confidence. "The best thing you can do is come to Charleston with me. I'll give you a job."

She knew it probably wouldn't work. They'd never gotten along very well. He was too bossy already, and to actually work for him day in and day out didn't bear thinking about. But he was offering her a way out of her humiliation. She desperately wanted to flee the entire situation, even though that would leave all the cleanup to her father and sister. She doubted they would mind, though. They loved her and would do anything for her. Besides, Hugh had tried to hide his true feelings, but she knew he'd never liked Robert. Naturally, he thought the world of Will.

Everyone who knew Will thought the world of him. He was tall, almost lanky, but with wide shoulders and well-muscled arms. He moved with incredible ease and grace for someone his size. His attitude was easy, too, as if life was a big joke and only he knew the punch line. No one meeting him for the first time would have guessed that he was the owner of two thriving art galleries, that in his office he was driven and dynamic.

His face was an artist's dream—wavy ash-blond hair combed back from his face and deep-set gray eyes under the thick eyebrows that seemed to be a trademark of his family. His face was long and narrow, ending in a squared-off chin. A sculptor, striving for perfection, might have rounded that jaw, realizing that no viewer of his work would believe anyone could have such a determined chin. Will had it, though, and the fortitude to go with it. She should know.

Throughout her college years in Columbia, Will had shown up regularly, ostensibly on business, but in truth to check up on her. She'd never quite understood why he had made himself her unofficial guardian, but he'd come frequently to take her out for a meal or to a movie. He had asked her about her classes, her roommates, friends, dates— especially her dates.

When she had objected to his nosiness, he'd said only that he was fulfilling a family obligation. It did no good to point out that they weren't family, because he would simply think up another reason to check on her every few weeks. It had continued until last year, when she had taken a job in Greenville and begun dating Robert.

Will had said very little about Robert except to give his halfhearted congratulations when she'd become engaged. Carrie cast Will a quick glance, wondering if he'd suspected Robert might not go through with the wedding.

At this moment, she could feel the powerful strength of Will's personality focused on her. His eyes were sharp and fierce, his head tilted at an angle that dared her to say no to his plan.

"Come with me," he said.

When she didn't immediately say yes, he let up on the gas pedal and guided the convertible to the side of the road. He coasted to a stop and let the motor idle. It was as if he was so strongly involved in bringing her around to his way of thinking, he wanted no distractions.

Carrie met his gaze and her mouth went dry.

It was crazy. Irresponsible. She couldn't do it. She opened her mouth to tell him so, but the look Will gave her was full of challenge, asking where her famous pride was.

Her voice squeaked when she tried to speak, and she had to clear her throat. "Everyone will think we're having an affair. That...that we've been having one the whole time Robert and I have been engaged."

Will shrugged. "So? Would you rather have people think you weren't good enough for one of the rich Gallatins to marry?"

"Certainly not!"

"Well, then, I dare you to face them down. Take my offer."

"This m—might not be the best time for me to be making such a decision."

"This is a one-time offer to save your pride. Take it or leave it," he responded arrogantly, then his face grew serious. "Tomorrow everything will be different. You know it will." He paused again. "I...I could use your help, Carrie."

Carrie wrestled with conscience and pride. Pride won. She took a deep breath. "All right, I'll do it, but stop at the first phone booth you see so I can call the church and tell Dad and Ginny the truth."

"Good girl," he said with approval. "You know, I was worried about you, especially when you get yourself engaged to that wuss Robert, but I think there may be hope for you yet."

"I can't tell you how that warms my heart," she answered.

Will laughed and shoved on the gas pedal.

They were almost out of town when he slowed and made a quick right turn. "I've got to stop at Sam's," he said, referring to his oldest brother. "He and Laura and little Travis will probably be on their way to the church by now. I know where their extra house key is hidden. You can call your dad from there while I get something from out back.''

"All right." Sadly, she looked at her beautiful gown. "Do you think Laura would mind if I borrowed some clothes and left this behind? I can't wear it all the way to Charleston, and, well, I think it's best if I don't go to Bret and Ginny's right now. There'll be people around.''

Will nodded and gave her a quick, approving look. "That sounds like a good idea. We can leave a note squaring it with Laura. I'm sure she won't mind.''

Within minutes, they pulled up in front of the big Victorian house where his brother and sister-in-law lived with their four-year-old son, Travis, and the hunting dogs Sam raised, trained and sold.

Carrie glanced around the neighborhood furtively as she stepped from the car and was grateful to see there seemed to be no one about. Will quickly found the house key where it was hidden under a table full of potted geraniums. He ushered Carrie inside and told her to meet him at the car when she was ready.

Carrie, who had visited the house often and babysat for Travis, knew where to find Sam and Laura's bedroom. Uncomfortable about looking through her friend's things, she was grateful to see a box marked for the church rummage sale in the upstairs hallway. She rousted out an old pair of slacks and a white T-shirt. Since Laura was several inches taller, Carrie had to roll up the legs of the slacks, and the shirt hung to mid-thigh, but she wasn't concerned about fashion. She'd spent hours this morning getting her hair and makeup exactly right, and look how much good that had done her!

After scribbling a quick note to Laura, she left the dress draped across a chair in Sam and Laura's bedroom.

Seeing it discarded so haphazardly made the sickness well up inside her once again, and she had to fight back tears. Questions still echoed through her mind as she touched the beautiful dress one last time. She slipped the big solitaire diamond ring from her finger and laid it on the dress. With a shaky breath, she closed the door on both items and headed downstairs to call the church.

It took several minutes for her to reach her father. Once she had explained the situation, Hugh was all for going after Robert with a shotgun.

"Dad," she said, hanging onto the phone desperately. "Tell everyone that Robert and I have decided not to get married, after all. I'm leaving town and I'll let you know when I get settled."

"Why? You've done nothing wrong! Come on back and face people down."

She wound the phone cord around her fingers until her knuckles turned white. Although she knew that was probably the best way to handle things, she couldn't do it right now. "I can't. Dad, I think my good judgment has been short-circuited by humiliation. Please try to understand. This isn't exactly the best day of my life!"

"All right, baby," he soothed. "Just let us know where to send your things."

"I'll—I'll be at Will's in Charleston."

"Will's? You mean Will Calhoun? What is it with these Calhoun men that they're always snatching my daughters away?"

"Dad, he's helping me out of an embarrassing situation. He's offered me a job, and I'm going to take it." It took another five minutes to persuade her father she was doing the right thing, but he finally agreed, assured her of his love and support and hung up the phone.

Carrie hurried out and saw Will waiting for her in the car. She locked the house, replaced the key and slipped into the seat beside him. He had put the top up on the car, but distracted by her own worries, she didn't see what he was holding until he turned and dropped a puppy into her lap—a fat little black furball about two months old.

"Is this what you were picking up?" she asked, scratching the animal behind his ears. The pup thanked her by licking her fingers.

Will started the motor and put the car into gear. "Yeah. He's a gift for my... for someone. I was going to pick him up after your wedding, but..."

"Since there's not going to be one, we'll take him with us now," she finished for him.

"No reason to wait."

"That's right," she agreed, but the firm nod she attempted wobbled, as did her bottom lip. Drawing a deep breath, she said, "Let's go."

# CHAPTER TWO

WITH a nod, Will pulled onto the street and headed for the highway. "Why don't you and the little guy there just try to relax? We'll be in Charleston by dinnertime."

Carrie took him at his word, settling into the bucket seat and taking comfort in the dog's warm weight nestled in her lap. They stopped a couple of times along the way for food or gas or to walk the puppy, but most of the time they rode in silence. Will, too, seemed to be lost in his own thoughts. Several times, he edged the speedometer well over the limit, but slowed each time she sent him an alarmed glance.

"Sorry," he said with an apologetic look. "I'm used to driving to please myself, but that'll have to change," he added in an undertone.

Carrie almost asked what was going to cause him to change his ways, but he was concentrating on his driving so she was content to keep quiet and observe him.

The family stories about Will's exploits had always fascinated her. Even though he worked hard, he always seemed to have time to squire some beautiful woman or another around town. Ginny and Bret had attended many of his gallery showings and been impressed by the glittering crowd and the prices people were willing to pay for the work his artists produced. Will's philosophy was that the appearance of success bred real success, and if he truly believed in an artist, he did everything he could for them.

He was dynamic and driven with a clear vision for what needed to be done—which had long been the source of the conflict between them. Never one to keep his opinions to himself, Will had insisted that Carrie was wasting her talents in advertising. He said she had a unique way of expressing herself and should be a writer. When she had protested, Will had asked if she was afraid to compete with the other writers in the family—her father and sister. Of course, Will was being ridiculous.

She had to admit that in spite of their frequent disagreements, she had always looked forward to Will's visits to her in college. By the time she had started her second year there, Will had opened the gallery in Charleston, then one in Columbia. Friends and family members had warned him that he was doing too much too soon, stretching his resources too thin, but he'd ignored them and forged ahead. Both galleries were soon prospering, and on his frequent visits to Columbia, he'd made it a point to see her.

Carrie had been delighted to go out with a successful man who happened to be fabulously attractive. His visits had prompted speculation and envy among her friends and roommates, and Carrie had never bothered telling them that the relationship was purely platonic—or that it was undeniably rocky.

It hadn't been easy, and she'd had to work very hard at it, but she'd managed to keep herself from falling in love with him by constantly reminding herself that a strong-willed, powerful man like him would not be a comfortable, reasonable mate.

Carrie shifted in her seat, disturbing the puppy, who gave her a sleepy-eyed look of curiosity before settling in her lap once again.

The problem with Will was that he wasn't a restful man, she thought. Take the way he drove, for instance—too fast and bordering on reckless, but he always managed to stay in control.

Funny. If someone had asked her which of the two men was more dependable, Robert or Will, she would have said Robert because he was quiet, a thinker. Stodgy, Will would have said. But she was wrong. Robert wasn't dependable at all, and Will had ridden to her rescue in his trusty white Mustang.

Her stomach clenched into a tight little knot of misery when she thought of Robert, and she squeezed her eyes shut to force back the tears.

Just about now, she should have been driving off on her honeymoon with her new husband. Instead, she was heading in the opposite direction with another man.

Carrie opened her eyes and studied Will's profile, the clearly defined nose, the sweep of his thick lashes. It would be easy for the citizens of Webster to believe she had thrown over Robert in favor of

Will. He was the kind of attractive, successful man any woman would like to run away with.

But, in spite of what Robert had done today, she didn't feel that her love for him had died an instant death. She wondered if it would take her longer to fall out of love than it had taken her to fall in. She felt sick at the thought.

She scooted down in the seat, clasped the puppy tightly and tried very hard to make her mind a blank. It must have worked, because she was surprised to find herself drifting into a restless sleep.

She woke, groggy and disoriented, when they pulled into Charleston, and she watched the lights of the beautiful city winking on as they made their way through the growing twilight.

When they pulled up before a rambling white house, she blinked and stretched. "Is this yours? I thought you lived in an apartment."

"I did." Will paused as if he wanted to say more. On the steering wheel, his hands opened and closed. He touched the control for the garage door opener, which was attached to the dash, and the big door before them rolled upward. "I had to buy a house."

"Probably a good investment," she said, glancing around vaguely.

"There were other reasons, which you'll see when we get inside."

Carrie gave him a puzzled look, but he didn't elaborate. She gathered up the puppy and stepped from the car. Glancing around, she saw that the garage was still crowded with boxes.

"Not quite moved in yet?" she said. "Will, if you don't have room for me, I can go to a hotel."

"Using what for money?" he asked with a quick grin as he plucked his suit jacket and the blue file folder from the backseat, and opened the door to the house. "You left your purse behind."

She glanced down and gave a helpless little laugh. "So I did. I hadn't noticed until now."

"Shock will do that to you." He paused in the doorway. "In fact, it can make you do many things you might not expect of yourself. Come on in."

Will pushed the door open for her, and she stepped into a spacious kitchen. A small birch dinette set stood in a bay window, which looked out on the backyard. "Not much furniture yet, I'm afraid, but I've got a bed for you."

Carrie followed him through the house, the ballet slippers she still wore silent on the tile and on the thick cream-colored carpet that covered the floor in the rest of the house. A faint noise at the back of the house had her pausing to listen. "Will, is that a kitten?" she asked. "Do you think it's a good idea to bring the puppy in?"

He shook his head. "It's not a kitten. Come on."

She followed him through the bare dining room and across the living room, which was sparsely furnished with two long leather-covered sofas and a couple of tables. They walked down a wide hallway with several doors leading off it. At the end, they entered what must have been the master bedroom.

Will strode into the room, but Carrie stumbled to a stop just inside the door when she saw that along with the usual furniture of bed, nightstands, and chest of drawers, which she had expected, there were two cribs along one wall.

A woman was seated in a rocking chair with a blanket-wrapped bundle in each arm. One of them was making a tiny mewling sound. Carrie, who had come home from college to help her sister for a couple of weeks after the births of her children, knew that sound.

"A baby?" she asked, sending Will a questioning glance.

"Two of them, actually," he said absently. He tossed the file folder onto the chest of drawers and approached the woman in the chair, who looked up in relief when she saw Will.

"Oh, Will. You're back early. Here," she said, indicating the burden in her arms. "I think the evening fussing is over, and these two are almost asleep, ready to be put to bed."

"I'll take care of it, Edith," he said. Scooping them up, he turned and said, "Edith Wiggins, this is Carrie McCoy. She'll be staying with us." His eyes went to the babies he held and he turned to show them to Carrie.

"Carrie, I'd like you to meet Ariana and Jacob. My children."

"Your . . . your *children?*" Carrie couldn't help it when her voice shot up.

"That's right. They're three weeks old." He glanced down, and his quick, intelligent eyes scanned the two tiny faces Carrie couldn't see. She witnessed concern as well as a deep glow of pride.

Carrie opened and closed her mouth a couple of times. She couldn't have been more surprised if he had suddenly revealed that he was setting off immediately to sail around the world on a raft.

"Children," she repeated in a flat, stunned tone. She went limp, nearly dropping the puppy. She made a grab for him and cradled him against her stomach. "Three-week-old babies. This...this is really a shock, Will. I don't know what to say." She shook her head, pressed her hand against her chest and blew out a sudden, surprised breath. "Twins. A boy and a girl. Whew!"

"Sh," Will cautioned. "Don't wake them." He was so absorbed in them, he barely seemed to notice that he'd left her on the point of hyperventilating.

Carrie tried to pull herself together, but she looked on in wide-eyed amazement as Will, the Calhoun family playboy, walked to one of the cribs. Bending his knees slightly, he placed one baby in it, then turned and placed the other one beside the first. From where she was standing, Carrie couldn't see which child was which. Their blankets were exactly the same shade of buttery yellow.

"I bought two cribs, but I always let them sleep together in the same one," he said, speaking over his shoulder to Carrie. "I saw a pediatrician on television who said twins are more comfortable this way at first."

He leaned with his forearm along the top crib railing, his shirt collar open and his sleeves rolled up. Both babies squirmed and cried softly. He attempted to quiet them by giving them a few endearingly awkward pats on the back.

Carrie remembered seeing his brother Bret doing the same thing to quiet one of his children. She felt an odd sort of warmth sift through her as she watched him. Somehow it was heartening to be part of this sweetly domestic scene. It made the shock she'd experienced that day fade a little.

Will looked up, catching her eye, seemingly waiting for something.

It took Carrie a few seconds to realize he expected an answer—even reassurance. "Oh, well, that makes sense," she said. "Since they've been so close together in their mother's womb, they should remain close."

Who *was* their mother? she desperately wanted to ask. And *where* was she? She kept quiet, though, because he was distracted by the children. Instead, she glanced at Mrs. Wiggins, who was eyeing the puppy asleep in Carrie's arms.

"You're sure a brave man, Will," the older woman said, shaking her head. "Two babies and a puppy. That's a load of work."

He glanced up. "That same pediatrician said it's good for kids to learn how to care for animals when they're young."

"As young as three weeks?" Carrie broke in, and the housekeeper sighed.

"Will, I signed on for daily work, not animal control."

Will shrugged off her mild complaint. "Don't worry, Edith. It'll work out." He ignored the lady's skeptical snort and said, "Why don't you show Carrie where the backyard is? She can let the little guy out there to explore his new home."

The housekeeper nodded. "Okay. Then I'll be on my way to *my* home. There's fresh formula in the refrigerator. Remember, if you warm it in the microwave, put it on low power, then stir it carefully so there aren't any hot spots or air bubbles."

"I'll remember."

The housekeeper turned and bustled out. "If you'll follow me, Miss McCoy, I'll show you where to take that animal."

Still half shocked, Carrie followed the brisk little woman. Once they reached the kitchen, she threw the back door open and indicated where the puppy was to be kept, all the time muttering under her breath about men who bit off more than they could chew.

Carrie was glad to see there was a bowl of water and one of puppy food along with a brand-new dog bed in one corner of the patio. There was nothing else around, further indication of the recentness of Will's move into the house. Had he bought the place and moved in specifically to have a bigger place for his children?

His children. The two words still nearly sent Carrie into shock. Surely his brothers didn't know about this, or someone would have mentioned it.

Mentioned it? Sam and Bret would have hurried to Charleston to see just what kind of situation their youngest brother had gotten himself into, and Laura and Ginny would have been right with them, asking questions and offering advice. And if Ginny had known, Carrie would have known, too. It wasn't the type of thing her sister would have kept secret.

She put the puppy down, and he waddled straight toward the dish of food. Although she didn't have many hopes that this arrangement would last very long, because the puppy was sure to get lonely and want company, she stepped inside. As she did so, she noticed that a small pet entrance had been installed in the bottom of the kitchen door. Will had assured her that the dog was thoroughly housetrained, but she had her doubts, because he was so young. At least, he could come and go as he pleased.

The housekeeper was picking up her purse in preparation for leaving. The light had been dim in the bedroom, so this was the first time Carrie was able to get a good look at her. She was small and wiry with softly curled short hair of silvery gray. Her eyes were lively and bright when she looked at Carrie and grinned. "Welcome to the house of surprises," she said. "We never know what's going to happen next."

"No kidding," Carrie answered. "Where... where is the children's mother? Asleep in another room, or..."

Mrs. Wiggins opened her purse and removed her car keys, then looked up with a slight frown. "You'd better let Will tell you about that himself." She turned toward the front of the house. "Good night."

Carrie, left alone in the kitchen, stared after her, wondering why the housekeeper was reluctant to talk. She turned and looked around with interest. The kitchen was charming, with richly shaded ash wood cabinets, new paint in sunny yellow and wallpaper splashed with sunflowers. In fact, although the home wasn't new, it smelled of fresh paint and new carpet. It was obvious that no expense had been spared in preparing the house for its new owners. It still had only the barest furnishings and few decorations on the walls. She speculated that the place might stay like this for a while. There would be little opportunity for decorating because Will's time would be torn between working and caring for the babies.

Babies. Carrie sat abruptly on a kitchen stool and eyed the wall phone. She was dying to call her sister and tell her about this.

Before she could reach for the phone, though, she heard Will's soft footfalls. He walked into the kitchen and stood looking around and blinking in the bright light, just as she had. She could see the lines of exhaustion on his face and wondered how she had missed them before. With two newborns at home, why had he made the drive to Webster for her wedding?

"I've only been a dad for three weeks," he said. "But I figure we've got twenty minutes tops before they wake up again. Are you hungry?" He swung the refrigerator open and grabbed a bottle of orange juice. He offered her some, and when she shook her head in refusal, he upended the bottle and chugged down several healthy swallows. Setting the bottle on the counter, he gave a gusty sigh and rolled his shoulders. He placed his hands loosely on his hips and gave her a curious look, as if asking her to begin shooting questions at him.

"Will, I'm not hungry for food, but I sure would like to ask a few questions," Carrie said. "Where did those babies come from?" When he grinned, she shook her head and said, "I didn't mean that the way it sounded. I *know* where babies come from. I mean, where is—"

"My wife?"

"You—you were married, too?"

A flash of amusement glinted in his eyes. "Yeah. I guess you could say I'm full of surprises today."

"No kidding."

The spark of humor faded from his expression. "Lani, my wife, died when Ariana and Jacob were born."

"Oh, Will," Carrie said with a gasp of dismay as she came instantly to her feet. She reached out to touch his arm in sympathy. "I'm so sorry. That must have been terrible for you."

"It was, but not in the way you think." Glancing to where her fingers rested on his forearm just below the rolled-up cuff of his shirt, he took her hand and held her fingers in his. His grip was strong, his long artist's fingers warm against hers.

He had held her hand this way many times before, though it had often been the prelude to an argument. This time, Carrie met his eyes and felt an unaccustomed flood of warmth spread through her. They'd both lost someone, and whether it was by death or design, losing still hurt.

"And I'm too tired to explain tonight," he went on. "I've got to sleep while they're sleeping." He dropped her hand, yawned and rubbed the back of his neck. "You know, I used to think it was a joke when Sam and Bret talked about learning to stay awake twenty-four hours a day when their kids were born, but it's no joke. Come on, I'll show you where your room is."

In the hallway leading to the bedrooms, he opened the door to a room furnished with a double bed, a chest of drawers and little else. "If you don't mind watching out for the puppy tonight..."

"No, not at all," she answered quickly. "You look dead on your feet."

"Yeah, I am. This wasn't how I expected to spend the day." He grimaced and gave her an apologetic look. "Of course, this isn't how you expected to spend the day—or the night, either."

"What?"

"Your wedding night," he prompted.

"Oh, no. No, it wasn't," she said, flustered.

He drew back in surprise. "Don't tell me you'd forgotten."

She took a deep breath. "Yes, for just a second there, I had. I can't believe it, but I had." It was all coming back now, though, pain followed by humiliation. She lifted her chin. "I'll go get the puppy and his bed and keep him in here with me. I hope he doesn't cry all night."

"Well, if he does, he'll only add to the chorus," Will said in a weary tone. He started for the door, then turned, pointing to the chest. "There are things in there I bought for Lani that she never used. In fact, she never even saw them. You might be able to find something to fit." He walked out, heading for his room.

Carrie went outside and brought the puppy in, along with his new bed. She settled him near her. His pudgy little body turned in circles as he tried to make himself at home in the pet basket. She gave him a dubious look as he sniffed and shuffled around, because she had the feeling he would be in bed with her before the night was over. He finally lay down, placed his head on his paws and gave her a mournful look as he whimpered low in his throat.

Carrie answered with a sympathetic smile and turned toward the chest of drawers. Feeling somewhat unnerved at the idea of going through the possessions of Will's late wife, she eased a drawer open and peeked inside.

The top drawer was full of plain cotton underclothing, still with the price tags attached. Packages of socks were tucked in beside them, unopened.

She closed the drawer carefully and looked in the next one. It was full of white and solid-colored cotton T-shirts and a couple of pairs of loose cotton slacks. The other drawers held nightgowns, nothing fancy, but their rich fabrics spoke of their quality. There was also a lightweight cotton robe.

Carrie considered the items for a few minutes, then closed the drawer carefully. There were no personal items, nothing faded or worn, no scent of a favorite perfume lingering on anything. Even the brush and comb on top of the chest looked brand new—and somehow the most disturbing.

In this day of shocks, these brand-new items were yet another strange twist. Will had said that Lani hadn't even seen them. Did that mean he had bought them and placed them in the dresser for Lani, who had then never returned from the hospital? Carrie found the thought sad and depressing, but speculating about Lani's fate kept her from dwelling on her own.

Carrie took a survey of the closet and saw three large cartons stacked inside. None of them was labeled, but she assumed the contents had belonged to Will's wife.

She placed her hand on one and thought about the woman whose belongings they must have been. Will had said his wife's death had been terrible for him, but not in the way Carrie thought. She wondered what he meant by that.

Closing the closet door, she returned to the dresser where she chose underthings and one of the T-shirts to wear as a nightshirt.

Quickly, she showered and prepared for bed. When she returned to the bedroom, she discovered that the puppy had gone quietly to sleep. Gratefully, she crawled into bed, determined to do the same, but she lay staring at the ceiling.

Although she was exhausted, sleep wouldn't come. The day's events kept playing over in her mind, from waking in her own room that morning, to Robert's note, to Will's stunning surprises.

She turned on her side and plumped the pillow under her cheek. No doubt about it. This was one wedding day she would never forget!

At first Carrie thought the soft mewling sounds she heard were coming from the puppy. Groggily, she rolled over and reached to comfort him, only to discover that he was sound asleep.

Still half-asleep, she pushed up onto her elbow and listened. The sound grew louder, and she realized it was one of the babies, then both of them.

She fumbled the light on and picked her watch up from the bedside table. One o'clock. Must be time for a feeding. Will would need her help.

She pulled on a pair of the slacks she'd seen in the dresser, and some socks, then smoothed her hair with both hands and padded down the hall to Will's room.

This time the room was well-lit, so it was easy for her to see Will bending over the crib, changing a diaper. Both babies were crying, and they seemed to be competing to see who could be the loudest.

Will must have sensed her standing in the doorway because he looked up. His brown hair was mussed, his eyes droopy with unsatisfied sleep and his jaw shadowed by beard, but he gave a pleased nod. "They slept three hours. That's pretty good."

Carrie smiled. He looked so hopeful, she couldn't bring herself to remind him that with babies that meant nothing. They might be awake for the next eight.

He had pulled on a pair of sweatpants and a T-shirt whose sleeves showed off the bulge of his muscles beneath the hems. She found it strangely disconcerting to see someone so masculine in such a domestic setting. She thought again about what an attractive man he was, then was confused by the conflicting feelings of disloyalty. How could she find any other man attractive when she was still in love with Robert?

Pushing those thoughts away, she walked up beside him. "Here, let me help."

He gave her a doubtful look, and she laughed softly. "If I can help with your niece and nephews, surely I can help with your children."

"Oh, yeah, I keep forgetting you baby-sat for Travis and stayed with Bret and Ginny for a while after Nancy and Brian were born."

"I'm an old hand at this," she assured him, finally glancing at the babies. She couldn't see much more of their faces than she had earlier, because they were both screwed up into furious scowls as they loudly protested the delay of their food.

Carrie took the diaper from Will. "Why don't you let me finish this while you get the bottles ready?"

He nodded and headed from the room. Jacob was freshly diapered, but Ariana still needed attention. Carrie took care of it quickly, then scooped both babies into her arms, being careful to support their heads and backs. Accustomed to the big babies

Ginny had borne, she was surprised at how tiny
Jacob and Ariana were. Together, they couldn't
have weighed much more than ten pounds.

They quieted for a few seconds because of the
change in their position, but when their bottles
weren't forthcoming, they started crying once again.

She walked around the room, bouncing them
gently and crooning softly, "It hurts to be hungry,
doesn't it? And it happens so often because your
tummies are so tiny. Well, just hold on for a little
bit. Your daddy's bringing your bottles. Don't
worry, he won't let you go hungry. He'll take good
care of you."

Barely aware of what she was saying, she continued her circuit of the room. She made a turn and
started in surprise when she saw Will standing in
the doorway, a baby bottle in each hand, his face
strangely intent as he looked at her. His gray eyes
were dark and narrowed as if he'd been drawn up
short by a startling thought. They swept over her,
from her feet in their clean, white socks, to her
tousled hair.

Carrie would have touched her hair self-
consciously if her arms hadn't been full. She knew
she looked a sight, but the expression on Will's face
made her think he wasn't really seeing her. She
couldn't quite decipher what his odd look meant.

"Will? Is something wrong?"

Her question seemed to snap him out of his pre-
occupation. He stepped forward. "Here," he said
briskly, handing her a bottle. "I'll feed Jacob if
you can handle Ariana."

"Of course," she said, taking the bottle from him as she studied his face, trying to discern what he had been thinking.

"You can have the rocking chair," he said, taking Jacob from her and seating himself on the side of the bed. "Sorry, I've only got the one rocking chair. I don't usually have help with this."

"What did you do, let one cry while you fed the other one?"

"Yeah," he said gruffly, but he didn't sound happy about it. He offered the bottle to Jacob, who began sucking lustily. "I had a nanny lined up, but her mother got sick and she was needed at home, so she couldn't take the job. Haven't found a replacement yet."

Carrie sat in the rocking chair and positioned Ariana in the crook of her arm. When she offered the bottle, Ariana turned her head frantically from side to side for a few seconds before latching onto the nipple. Instantly, she quieted and began nursing.

The silence was instant and welcome. With a sigh, Carrie began rocking slowly. She glanced up to see that Will had relaxed against the headboard. His head fell back to rest on the carved wood, and his eyes closed briefly.

Carrie admired the strong column of his neck, his wide, flat shoulders and the muscles in his upper arms that reminded her of cannonballs. The sight of him holding a baby against those hard muscles and a bottle in his wide hand should have appeared incongruous, but instead it seemed right. Mentally, she compared him to Robert, who had a slim build and a quiet manner. Funny, she'd always thought she preferred that type of man. She'd believed Robert would have made a good father, but now she wondered if fathering would have come as easily to him as it did to Will, and. . . .

Oh, lord, she was doing it again. Having the most inappropriate thoughts at the most inappropriate time.

She didn't know why she was comparing the two men. She hadn't given Will much thought except for the times he'd irritated her by giving out unasked-for advice.

Maybe she was spending so much time thinking about him because he had whisked her out of Webster and brought her to his home, where she was seeing a new side of him.

Shaking her head, she sat up straighter, disturbing Ariana, who released the bottle's nipple and let out a tiny wail. Carrie settled the baby once again, then glanced up to see that Will's eyes were open and watching her.

"Will, why didn't you call your family for help? Laura or Ginny would have come if they'd known."

He lifted an eyebrow at her. "They were involved in wedding preparations, remember?"

"Oh, yes, of course." Embarrassed, she concentrated on lifting Ariana and placing her against her shoulder to burp her. "But, still, you could have at least told them what was going on."

"They would have insisted on coming. You know they would have. I was planning to tell Sam and Bret right after the wedding. That's why I went to

Webster yesterday. I was going to get together with them right after you and your groom drove away into the sunset. It seemed like the kind of thing that needed to be said face-to-face, and since Mrs. Wiggins was willing to take care of them all day, it seemed like a good time to go."

One corner of Carrie's mouth lifted in an ironic smile. "Oh, you weren't really coming to my wedding, then?"

"I would have been there," he said, his voice gruff. "But thank God, I didn't have to be."

# CHAPTER THREE

"WHAT do you..."

"Better put a diaper on your shoulder, Carrie. Ariana's the one who spits up." He glanced down at Jacob. "This guy, on the other hand, never gives anything up."

Carrie did as he suggested, burping Ariana, then offering her more formula. The baby had lost interest, though, and was drifting off to sleep. Standing carefully, Carrie replaced her in the crib, turning her on her side and propping her, front and back, with small blankets doubled into rolls to support her. The baby made a few whimpering sounds, and Carrie patted her in comfort.

"So that's how you do it," Will muttered. "The pediatrician on television said to put them on their backs or on their sides for sleeping, but I couldn't quite figure out how to do that side thing."

"I learned it from Ginny," Carrie answered, taking Jacob from him and positioning him in the same way. When he let out a wail, Carrie began rubbing the tip of her finger back and forth above his eyebrows. Within a few minutes, his eyelids seemed to grow heavy and he went to sleep.

Will sighed when both babies settled down. "You sure seem to know what you're doing. I usually have to walk the floor with them for an hour after each feeding. Must need a woman's touch," he added in a low tone.

Carrie smiled as she reached into the crib to pull their yellow blanket over them. "No, Will. I've just had a little more experience at this than you have, that's all."

"You'd think I'd remember a few things from when my sisters were babies, but I don't. I guess I'll learn," he said around a huge yawn. He rubbed his face and pressed the heels of his hands against his eyes. Then he rolled his shoulders and glanced at Ariana's bottle. "How much formula did she take?"

Carrie picked it up and squinted. "Less than two ounces."

"Then she'll be awake again in no time." He took both bottles, returned them to the kitchen and was back in a few minutes.

"You need to get some sleep," Carrie said, frowning at him. "I can stay in here, sleep in the rocking chair and take care of Ariana when she wakes up, or you could go in my room to sleep."

"Or you could join me on this bed."

She straightened, blinking at him. "What?"

"Don't look so shocked," he said with a faintly mocking grin. "We're going to be up again in a little while. It makes sense for us to sleep together."

Something about the way he said it made her insides go still and her mouth turn dry. "I can hear them from my room."

"You can hear them better from here." His eyes were steady on hers, and even though he hadn't moved a muscle, she felt as if he had reached out and tugged her to him.

She ran her palms down her thighs. "I'm sure I could, but the puppy—"

"Can find his way out of your room if he needs us."

"Oh, well, I suppose so," she said, giving the door, and the escape it offered, a longing glance.

"Are you saying this is as much help as you're going to offer for one night?"

Immediately, guilt twisted her heart. "Well, no, of course not. It's obvious you need help, and—"

"Then lie down with me, Carrie." He held out his hand and made a sweeping gesture toward the king-size bed.

The way he said it sent a shiver skipping up her spine, but his request made perfect sense. She was being ridiculous—building something into this that he certainly didn't mean.

Or did he? She noted the sensual slant to his eyes and the tiniest curve to his lips, but she couldn't refuse his request.

Watching him, she moved to the side of the bed opposite him and pulled back the covers. Slipping inside, she arranged the pillow under her head and pulled up the blanket.

Will turned out the light and climbed into bed beside her. The wide mattress dipped with his weight, then settled. Carrie felt a surge of distress, then longing, and she couldn't have said which was the more disturbing because she didn't understand the reason for either.

Ruthlessly, she shoved all thoughts aside. She was emotionally and physically exhausted. This wasn't the time to be second-guessing herself. She needed rest, and if she had to rest in Will Calhoun's bed, then so be it.

Will's low voice rumbled in the darkness. "Good night again, Carrie."

"Good night, Will," she answered, surprised at the amount of comfort she drew from the sound of his voice. She began to relax, her thoughts finally beginning to slow and drift as she teetered on the edge of sleep.

In fact, she was so close to sleep that she could almost have convinced herself it was a dream when she heard Will's faint chuckle.

"Who'd have thought I would get little Carrie McCoy into bed with me on her wedding night?"

Carrie came awake to the scent of coffee perking, but her mind was too foggy to wonder where it was coming from. She felt warm and comfortable even though her head seemed to be resting on a rock. She didn't want to move it quite yet, though, so she let her thoughts drift lazily. Ariana had awakened twice more during the night, and Jacob once. Carrie and Will had shared the feeding duties and floor-walking time. Will had commented again that he was grateful to have her help because it made things easier for him. Since he insisted on getting up with the babies even if she was handling the feeding, she didn't see how she was making it easier for him, but she didn't argue.

If she had been the one sitting in the rocking chair, giving one of the babies a bottle, he would prop himself against the headboard of the bed and watch her. He said he was studying her technique so he could pick up pointers.

But he didn't seem to practice those pointers. If he was the one doing the feeding, his attention seemed to be equally divided between Carrie and the infant he was tending.

It was her face he watched, as if he was trying to discover what she was thinking. Maybe he feared that she was thinking about Robert and the humiliation of their almost wedding. Certainly, it would have been natural if she had been, but somehow during the long night hours when everything seemed so surreal, it wasn't Robert who had been on her mind, but Will and his children.

She recalled what he'd said about getting little Ginny McCoy into bed with him on her wedding night and felt a flush climb her cheeks. She wasn't even going to speculate on what he'd meant, although she decided that it probably had been a good idea for them to share the bed. It had given her comfort she had badly needed at the time.

That made her think of Robert, and she suppressed a groan of pain. Like a surgeon probing a wound, she examined her feelings and discovered that it hurt as much on this new day as it had the day before. The tears she should have shed were locked inside her. She wasn't ready to release them, or to face the hurt and deal with it, though, so she focused her mind on Will once again.

The hard object beneath her head moved, and Carrie realized with a start that it was Will's shoulder. She was snuggled up to his side, and his arm was around her.

Carrie's eyes sprang open, and she stared at him. Her mind must have been truly fogged for her not to have realized that he was holding her. Never could she have imagined herself in such an intimate position with Will, but she took it as further proof that everything in her life had been turned upside down.

They had done nothing more than share the bed, but somehow he had reached out to her in the night, and she had gone willingly to him.

It should have been Robert holding her. She should be waking up with her new husband in a honeymoon suite at a resort on Hilton Head Island. She should be looking forward to a day of lazing on the beach with Robert, long walks in the moonlight, tennis, golf, whatever couples did on their honeymoon besides spend hours making love. Instead, she was in bed with Will Calhoun.

And to add to her confusion, it felt unnaturally right.

She should move away, Carrie thought with a surge of distress. She *intended* to move away, but she found herself tilting her head carefully and studying his face.

He was sound asleep, his breathing deep and even. In the morning light, she could see his long, dusky lashes lying against his cheekbones and the shadow of early morning beard that stubbled his jaw. The night of disturbed sleep had only served to deepen the lines of exhaustion etched into his face. She wanted to lift her hand and smooth those lines with her fingers, to ease some of his burden, but she dared not touch him.

She was very conscious of his hand lying possessively across her waist. If she reached up, touched him, made a gesture of affection or caring, it would be like sealing the two of them together somehow. She would be closing the circle of need.

And she wasn't ready for that.

Had she snuggled up to him in the night, imagining, or worse, pretending, that he was Robert? Carrie cast that thought aside as soon as it formed. No. There was no way she could have confused the two men.

She thought she still loved Robert despite the way he'd jilted her. She didn't love Will. The fact that she found him attractive, virile and sexy didn't mean that her mind was substituting him for Robert. After all, she'd always known that about Will, but she'd never let it affect her before.

Carrie eased away from him and slipped from the bed. On tiptoe, she made a quick check of the crib where the twins were sleeping peacefully.

Her lips curved into a soft smile when she looked at their angelically untroubled faces. They were such beautiful children, it made her wonder what their mother had looked like. She must have had dark hair and eyes because her children did.

They would be real standouts at the next Calhoun family get-together. These two would be contrasts to the other Calhoun children, who were blonds. In fact, Brian was a real cotton top with hair that was almost platinum.

Jacob and Ariana were perfect in their own way, though, she thought, with a surge of possessiveness that surprised her. With Will taking care of them, they would grow up healthy and strong. No doubt they would be people who would have made their late mother proud.

Carrie's smile grew into a grin. It would help if they learned to sleep through the night so their father would have the energy to raise them.

One way or another, they had kept the adults awake most of the night, and now that it was time to wake up, they couldn't be more sound asleep.

It was going to be a while before these two worked themselves into any kind of normal schedule, she thought as she left the room.

In her own room, she discovered that the puppy was gone. She only hoped he'd found his way outside and hadn't left any unpleasant little surprises in the house. She dressed in butter yellow slacks and T-shirt from the stock Will had bought for his wife, then followed the inviting coffee aroma down the hall to the kitchen.

She poured herself a cup of the dark brew, took a sip and headed to the refrigerator for milk, which she poured in with a liberal hand. She smiled as she took another sip. Edith certainly knew how to brew coffee to suit Will.

Carrie stepped to the back window, where she stood sipping as she watched the puppy nosing around the backyard. He was a cute little mutt, but she couldn't imagine why Will wanted to take on a puppy as well as two babies. The house of surprises, Edith had called Will's home, and it certainly lived up to that description. She hoped that today she would find out the reasons behind those surprises.

Turning, she carried her coffee with her into the laundry room, where the housekeeper was busy folding tiny nightgowns and bootees and placing them in stacks.

She gave Carrie's sleepy face a swift, critical look, then smiled. "Ah, the walking wounded. Good morning."

Ginny smiled. "Do I look that bad, Edith?"

"No, considering you probably got drafted into floor-walking duty and didn't sleep more than a few hours, you look pretty good."

"I was crazy enough to volunteer for duty," Ginny answered, taking another sip of coffee.

"Hey, it wasn't that bad," Will said from behind her. "They actually had a peaceful night."

Carrie turned to glance at him and saw that he'd showered, shaved and dressed in a fresh shirt and faded jeans, but through her mind flashed the memory of how he'd looked stubble-cheeked and relaxed in sleep. She felt a soft, slow tingle spread through her chest. Frowning, she glanced down, wondering if she was drinking her hot coffee too fast.

"I hoped you'd sleep a little longer," she said.

His gray eyes gave her a swift look. "I intended to, but I've got to go into the gallery later, and we need to talk."

She nodded, hoping he meant he was going to answer her questions. Better yet, maybe he was ready to tell her about the job he had for her at his galleries. It would be great to concentrate on plans and not on yesterday's fiasco.

"That sounds like a good idea," she said. "But maybe I'd better go check on Jacob and Ariana first. They might need something."

"I'll go," the housekeeper said, filling her arms with freshly washed baby clothes and starting from the room. "I need to put these away. You two can be on your own for breakfast. I'll see to the babies." She paused in the doorway. "Oh, by the way, a Ginny Calhoun has called twice, but she said not to wake you. I assume she's a relative?"

Carrie smiled, imagining the questions her sister would have for her. "She's my sister and Will's sister-in-law."

"I see. She said she'd call back later."

"I don't doubt that for a second," Will murmured, then he gestured for Carrie to precede him out of the room. "Let's go eat breakfast so I can tell you everything you need to know before you call Ginny back. That way she can spread the news and the whole family can descend on us by the weekend," he finished on a long-suffering note.

Carrie followed him and made toast while he set out boxes of breakfast cereal and a carton of milk. They ate at the table in the sunny alcove. Will finished before she did, poured himself another cup of coffee, then began without preamble to answer the questions that had bothered her all night.

"Ariana and Jacob are my children legally, but not biologically."

Carrie set down the triangle of toast she'd been spreading with strawberry jam. She'd lost interest in it. "Go on," she invited.

"Their mother, my wife—" he hesitated as if the word was strange on his tongue "—Lani Gray was an artist whose work I represented. She was twenty years old, brilliantly creative. She painted in oils, intricate canvases full of dark colors and tortured imagination, but her output was erratic, so her income was, too."

"Was she... troubled?" Carrie asked, then gave him an embarrassed look. That wasn't the kind of thing she should be asking about his wife, for goodness' sake.

Will didn't seem to take offense, though he gazed at her for a few seconds, frowning deeply. "Troubled and very ill. She was diabetic and didn't take care of herself. She'd been in the hospital more than once when she couldn't control her blood sugar. When she got pregnant, she didn't see a doctor for fear he would recommend an abortion because of the diabetes. She was young and in a panic. In fact, she didn't see a doctor until she was in her sixth month."

Carrie stared and shook her head. "She was taking a terrible chance."

Will gazed out the window. "She took a great many chances. She hoped that she could hold her boyfriend, a biker with the revolting single name of Sledge, by having a baby, but he skipped out as soon as she told him she was expecting. The coward jumped on his Harley and took off. He's probably in California somewhere, sweet-talking some other naive young girl."

Carrie felt a sudden pain as if someone had taken her heart and given it a cruel twist. Her abandonment was fresh in her mind. With careful concentration, she picked up her coffee cup.

"The bastard couldn't live up to his responsibility. The big, tough guy didn't even leave her a message." Will snorted in derision. "Of course, there's always the chance the idiot doesn't know how to write. Coward," he muttered again.

Hearing the echo of what he had said about Robert the day before, Carrie felt the color drain from her face. Her hand dropped, rattling her cup against the saucer.

Will's head snapped around, and his sharp eyes took in her pale face. He sat forward and wrapped his hand around hers. "Damn, Carrie, I'm sorry. I'm an insensitive jerk."

She took a breath, but her throat felt full, as if tears were damming up somewhere deep inside and threatening to break through. "It's... it's all right. Go on with what you were saying."

"I was saying that Sledge couldn't keep his word, and he ran off."

"He may have had a good reason," Carrie began lamely, but her tongue stumbled over itself when Will gave her a sour look.

"There's never a good reason to leave a sick, pregnant woman with no family, few resources, no health insurance and little means of support."

"No." Carrie fiddled with her cup, tilting it until the coffee sloshed near the rim, then righting it. "No, of course not."

She knew what he was thinking as clearly as if he had said the words aloud—that Lani's boy-friend was no different than Robert. She could have answered that the women were certainly different. She, at least, was healthy and could support herself.

Carrie pulled her thoughts away from her own hurt for a second and considered Will. She couldn't imagine him abandoning his responsibility. In fact, he'd taken on another man's.

With a flash of insight, Carrie realized that was why he was so hard on Robert and why he was so impatient with her reluctance to condemn Robert.

"You married Lani to take care of her?" she prompted, though what she really wanted to know was whether he'd been in love with the girl. He must have had some affection for her to have married her.

"Yes, she needed someone and I was the closest thing she had to a friend. Besides being sick and pregnant, she'd had a fire in her apartment. She wasn't home at the time, but she lost almost every-thing. The shock put her in the hospital. While she was there, I bought this house and furniture for her and the babies, and we were married by the hospital chaplain. Ariana and Jacob were born a month early, weighing four pounds apiece.''

As he spoke, his voice was steady and even-toned, and Carrie marveled at it. He must have gone through agonies of worry, but she knew he'd probably never doubted he was doing the right thing.

It was typical of the Calhoun men. They were sure of themselves, and often sure they knew what was best for everyone else, too. Until this moment, she hadn't considered that to be a particularly good thing.

Carrie felt a sudden prickle across the back of her neck as she realized that in the past twenty-four hours, her perception of Will had undergone a dramatic change. Many thoughts and feelings hit her at once—surprise, respect—and the uncomfortable realization that she had known this man for almost five years, yet she didn't really know him at all. It was a minute before she could collect herself to ask, ''So ultimately, Lani's death was caused by diabetes?''

''She slipped into a diabetic coma after the babies were born. We hoped she would pull out of it, but her body had been through too much. It couldn't recover.''

The tears that had been threatening since yesterday welled and spilled over. Reaching out, she touched his hand. ''Oh, Will, I'm so sorry. Did...did she get to see her babies before she...''

"No. She never regained consciousness. That was the hardest part," he said grimly. "Because she'd fought so hard to carry them—to have them. You see, she was orphaned when she was ten. Her parents died in a boating accident, and she grew up in foster homes. She had no one to love her, no one to love. That's why she was so desperate to have the babies." His lips quirked. "You should have seen how excited she was when she learned she was having twins."

Carrie's fingers fumbled a paper napkin out of the ceramic holder on the table. She sniffled unashamedly into it. "That poor girl. That poor, poor girl," she said, her voice clogged with tears. After a minute, she mopped her eyes. "Oh, Will, that's the saddest thing I've ever heard, and it was just three weeks ago. How did you stand it?" She looked up, her caramel-colored eyes awash in tears.

"Ariana and Jacob needed me. I had to concentrate on them."

"Of course you did," she agreed.

Will sat gazing into his cup, giving Carrie an opportunity to study him. His gray eyes were dark with his thoughts. There were many more questions she wanted to ask him, but she hesitated. She wasn't sure how much of this she could take in at one time. Finding out he had children had been a surprise, but she hadn't guessed the depth of his commitment to them.

She should have guessed, though. Will came from a long line of men who lived up to their responsibilities. Their father had died when Sam was fifteen

Bret ten and Will only six. They had banded together to take care of their mother and two younger sisters, Beth and Lisa.

Carrie crossed her arms and leaned forward, gazing at him. How was it that she hadn't seen this in him before? They had spent a great deal of time together over the years. Was it possible she'd been so wrapped up in herself that she hadn't bothered to know him at all? That didn't speak well for her.

"After the fire, when Lani was hospitalized, the doctors thought right away that she might not make it through delivery," Will went on. "A hospital social worker said arrangements had to be made for the babies. He told me that since she had no next of kin, they would be put into a foster home if she didn't make it. Even though there are long waiting lists for adoptable babies, he wasn't sure of their chances of being adopted because of their mother's medical history and lack of prenatal care."

Carrie pressed her lips together, willing away fresh tears. The situation Will was describing made her jilting seem like a minor inconvenience in comparison.

"Were you...were you the one who had to tell her all this?" she asked, but she already knew the answer. Of course, he had been. It wasn't the kind of thing he would have left to someone else, even Lani's doctor.

"Yes, and I suggested right away that we should be married so the kids would have a father as well as a mother."

"Even though you thought their mother might not live?"

"Yeah," Will answered with an ironic lift of his dark brows. "The truth is, I knew she wouldn't make it. I guess you could say I had a feeling about it. But we did it, and in a matter of days, I was a father."

"And a widower."

"Yes," Will said again. "Not the way I expected fatherhood to happen to me. Strange how life can throw curves at you."

"No kidding," Carrie answered with a fervent sigh.

Will gave an ironic little laugh. "I guess after yesterday you're pretty much an expert on that," he admitted. He stood suddenly and walked to the sink where he rinsed his cup and set it on the counter. "I've got to get to work. I've hardly been in the office in the past month, and my gallery manager tells me the work's piled up to the rafters, but I'll try to be home early. Can you help Edith today?"

"Of course." She rose hastily to hurry through the house after him. "But Will, what about the job you said you had for me?"

"We can talk about that this evening. You don't need to jump right into a new job after what you've been through."

Irritation flared within her, but she kept it in check and tried to use a reasonable tone of voice. "I don't need to be coddled. I need a job."

He cocked an eyebrow at her in a gesture she'd always found particularly irritating. "You've got a job, Carrie, recovering from the emotional shock of having that wuss Robert leave you standing at the altar," he growled.

Carrie clamped her hands onto her waist. "Oh, nicely put, Will."

"I'm not one to mince words."

"How well I know that," she muttered, giving him a sour look. She knew that losing her temper would do no good. Will was sure he was right, as usual.

This situation had a familiar ring to it. It was exactly like the discussions they used to have when he would drop by to see her during her college years. However, she couldn't let Will think he was going to run her life—even if he had helped her save her pride yesterday, and despite the tender feelings she'd just been having about what he'd done for Lani.

He started from the room, and she stalked along right behind him. "Will," she persisted. "I need to begin making plans. I'm not the type to sit around all day and do nothing."

He turned to her with a wry glance. "With newborn twins in the house? Believe me, you'll be plenty busy. In fact, you'll probably be more tired than I'll be by dinnertime."

Carrie acknowledged that was probably true, but she was thinking up fresh arguments when she heard a cry from the bedroom. She forgot what she was going to say and hurried to see what was wrong.

Edith was tending to Ariana while Jacob cried lustily, pulling his legs up and kicking them out in his fury at being denied immediate attention. Carrie hurried over and scooped him up, speaking softly to him while Will looked on.

"See what I mean?" he said dryly.

Carrie merely gave him a look as she cradled Jacob against her shoulder and watched Will take a tie from the closet, flip up his collar and knot it carefully around his neck.

Carrie looked around the room, noting that Edith had made the bed and tidied up. She gave the woman a quick glance. She wondered if the housekeeper had noticed that two people had shared the bed last night.

Will shrugged into his suit jacket, then opened his dresser drawer and removed the file folder he'd put there the night before. He placed it in his briefcase, clicked the locks down, then grasped the handle.

He crossed the room, took Ariana from Edith and gave her a kiss, then handed her back. Murmuring about preparing the babies' baths, Edith carried the tiny girl from the room.

Approaching Carrie, who was holding Jacob with one hand cradling his little bottom and the other one cupped around the back of his head, Will laid his hand across Jacob's back. Carrie noted that his fingers could have wrapped all the way around to the front of the baby's tiny chest, but his touch was feather-light.

Leaning in, Will kissed Jacob's cheek. His lips also skimmed across Carrie's fingers, and she had to fight the sudden urge to shiver. The faint scent of his cologne teased her, and she drew in a quick breath.

Hearing her, Will's eyes lifted and met Carrie's over the baby's downy head, and his hand slipped down to cover hers. He gave it a slight squeeze as if he thought she was as fragile as his tiny son.

"We'll talk tonight, Carrie," he said, and she knew there would be no more discussion about it. He didn't exert the slightest bit of pressure on her flesh, but she felt as if he was imprinting himself on her.

Her body gave in to the need that she'd been fighting as a shiver passed through her. He must have felt it, because she saw a quick flash of interest in his eyes, as if he was intrigued by her reaction.

"Tonight, Carrie," he said and waited until she dipped her chin in agreement.

With a nod, he strode from the bedroom, leaving Carrie clutching his son and wondering what she'd just agreed to.

# CHAPTER FOUR

"I COULDN'T believe it when Dad came and told us what Robert had done, Carrie." Ginny Calhoun's agitated voice came over the phone and bounced against her sister's eardrum. Carrie held the receiver away and grimaced.

"Yes, well, it came as a surprise to me, too."

The irony in her tone was lost on Ginny, who had a fine head of steam going and wouldn't slow down until she'd released some of her anger against Robert Gallatin.

"You should have seen his parents' faces. They looked as if they'd been stabbed."

"Oh, no," Carrie murmured in dismay. She'd forgotten all about Robert's parents. She'd always liked them, and they had liked her. She hated to think of them being hurt. "You mean he didn't tell them, and they were sitting right there with everyone else?"

"That's right. Dad waited until everyone was seated before he made the announcement so he'd only have to say it once. I happened to be looking at the Gallatins at the time, and oh, their faces were just sick. It seems that the only person he told was his sister, Marcia. Of course, the Gallatins think it's all your doing—that you dumped him to run off with Will."

Carrie rubbed her forehead. "Having Dad say that seemed like a good idea yesterday, but I never meant to hurt Robert's parents."

"I know, but I'm wondering if that's what Robert intended."

"What do you mean?"

Ginny paused for a minute, then said, "Oh it just seems that he could have been a little more considerate of their feelings. After all, he's their only son, and they've always babied him."

That was true, Carrie admitted to herself, but she hadn't let herself think of it as a problem. In fact, she hadn't given much thought to the relationship she and Robert would have with his parents. She'd been so involved with the details of the wedding that she'd let other considerations slip by.

Ginny rushed on. "So, anyway, Laura and I went straight over to your house—I mean Robert's house and packed up all the wedding gifts we could find. Thank goodness you had the house key in your purse—how did you manage to leave your purse behind, by the way? We found a complete list of who sent what gifts. We're returning them all."

"Thanks, Sis. I'm sure that's best," Carrie said.

"I don't mind telling you everyone was shocked. The gossip is still buzzing around town. Nancy was heartbroken because she didn't get to be flower girl."

Regret leveled in Carrie's stomach. "Tell her I'll make it up to her. When I get my own place, she can come stay with me for a few days this summer."

That is if she could get time off from the job that had yet to materialize.

"I'll tell her. As for Robert, all I can say is that Dad, Bret and Sam are ready to kill him, except that nobody can seem to locate him."

Carrie sat up straight. "What do you mean?"

"I mean he's disappeared. Not that Laura and I expected to see him at his house yesterday. Even his parents and Marcia don't seem to know where he is. He gave Marcia that note yesterday morning, then left town. His father said he's going to come out of retirement and return to run the family's furniture stores. From what I hear, Robert called Mr. Gallatin to say he'd be gone for a while, but he didn't say where he was calling from. The silly coward."

"That's exactly what Will calls him."

"Speaking of Will, how did he happen to be Johnny-on-the-spot and manage to convince you to go all the way to Charleston with him?"

"He promised me a job."

"Well, I guess that's good, but don't you think you'd be happier here at home, with me to take care of you?"

Carrie sighed. She had expected this offer from her sister. "You've mothered me since I was five years old, Ginny. I've got to stand on my own two feet sometime. Besides, I'm needed here."

Carrie glanced down. The debacle of her wedding seemed to fade a little as she fondly examined the babies, who were asleep in their infant carriers. She was seated on a kitchen stool with her feet propped on the rungs and her elbow resting on the counter.

After their morning feeding, she and Edith had bathed them, and while Edith took care of the housework, Carrie had played with them, rocked them to sleep, then fed them again. She had stretched out on Will's bed for a nap and felt ready to face another night with them.

Now that it was late afternoon, she had set them near the sliding glass doors to the patio so they could take a look outside.

The big wide world into which they'd been born didn't interest them very much, however. They had both dropped off to sleep within minutes. The puppy had wandered in and taken an exploratory sniff of the two little people. Apparently he'd liked the way they smelled because he had flopped down at their feet to join them in a nap. The three of them made such a peaceful scene that Carrie wished she had a camera to take their picture for Will.

Since things were quiet at the moment, Edith had gone to do the grocery shopping before starting dinner, leaving Carrie in charge.

"Needed for what?" Ginny demanded. "What does Will have for you to do? You don't know anything about the art gallery business."

"I can learn," Carrie said, bridling at Ginny's big-sister-knows-best tone. "But right now I'm taking care of his children."

Carrie could almost hear the hissing sound as Ginny's temper cooled down abruptly. After a moment, she said, "His what? This must be a bad connection. I thought you said his children."

Carrie grinned. "The connection's just fine. I did say children. Will has twins, a boy and a girl, three weeks old. He thought you and Bret might like to come down this weekend to meet them. Sam and Laura are welcome to come, too."

Ginny let out a squeak of surprise, which made Carrie laugh. Ginny thought Carrie was trying to play a joke on her, and it took several minutes of explanations to convince her she was telling the truth. While Ginny was stunned into speechlessness, Carrie gave her a list of items she needed from the cartons of things she had boxed and stored at Ginny's after giving up her Greenville apartment. She had planned to move them into Robert's house after the honeymoon, but now she was glad she hadn't.

The conversation finally ended, and she laughed again as she heard Ginny calling for her husband even before she had broken the connection.

Hanging up the phone, Carrie swiveled around on the stool and gazed at Jacob and Ariana. Their sweet innocence drew her to sit on the floor beside them. She touched their hands to make sure they were warm enough, though considering the June heat, she didn't know why she was worried.

They were such beautiful babies. That morning, while bathing them, she had examined them carefully, delighted to see that, in spite of their rocky start in life and the premature birth, they were perfectly formed. In fact, as far as she could tell, they were perfect in every way.

At last, she let her hand fall on the puppy, who managed to crank one eye open, give her an uninterested look and let it slam shut again.

"We need to find you a name, little guy," she said softly. "Something that fits your personality—like Sleepy or Sloth."

She scratched behind his ears as she thought about all her sister had told her. Now that she'd had a day to get her perspective, she regretted running off so hastily and leaving all the cleanup to others. Ginny didn't seem to mind, though. It was giving her a way to work off her anger toward Robert. Carrie knew she should have stayed in Webster to do the same thing. Taking down the decorations at the church, sending back the gifts and dealing with the questions would have given her a sense of closure, even though the question of why Robert had jilted her still went unanswered.

Thinking about him gave her a physical ache around her heart, and she wondered how long it was going to take her to fall out of love with him.

If only she had some clue as to why Robert had done it, she could find the closure she needed. Other than the reluctance to talk that he'd shown in the past few weeks, she couldn't recall any problems. Although he was several years older than she was, they'd always had a great deal in common. He was easy to be with, quiet and thoughtful. Not like Will, who challenged her at every step.

She frowned, trying to recall when the change in Robert had begun, but could only pinpoint that it had started when he'd returned from a business trip to Atlanta in late April, though she didn't know what that could have to do with it.

Her gaze fell on the children once again. How nice to enter the world so pure and untouched, with nothing but possibilities ahead of them. She experienced a fierce tug of hope that nothing would ever hurt these two. She knew that Will was going to be a wonderful father and would do everything in his power to protect them, but even he might not be completely successful.

It would be very easy for her to fill her broken heart with love for Jacob and Ariana.

Thinking of the children, and realizing she might never have any of her own because it would be a long time before she was willing to trust someone enough to love again, Carrie's tears finally came. Sorrow over the loss of Robert, anger at his cowardice and betrayal and embarrassment all washed over her in a wave. Tears gushed from her eyes, and she made a hasty grab for the clean cloth diaper she had draped across the back of Ariana's infant seat.

These tears were different than the ones she'd shed for Lani. These were purely self-pity, and she knew it, but she needed to do this just once. She stayed huddled on the floor for several minutes, quietly sobbing out her pain and sorrow.

"Thinking about your errant bridegroom?"

With a startled gasp, Carrie turned her head to see Will, briefcase in hand, standing at the end of the kitchen counter. His tie was loosened, his jacket was thrown over his shoulder, and his face held a ferocious scowl.

Her hand flew to her chest. "Will, you scared me out of my wits." She gave her eyes a last hasty swipe. "I . . . I didn't hear you come in."

"Too busy indulging in your pity party, hm?"

"I wasn't!" She flared immediately, but her protest died. She'd already admitted to herself that was exactly what she'd been doing, but she'd be darned before she would admit it to Will.

With as much dignity as she could pull together, she rose to her feet and dusted off the seat of her slacks.

While she was taking the last few unnecessary pats to her backside, Will said, "Dr. Paul says if you want happy children, they should be in a happy atmosphere. If you're going to cry like that, maybe you should go to your room."

Lifting her chin, she asked, "Who is Dr. Paul?"

Will's gray eyes sharpened as he examined her puffy eyes and defiant expression. "Television pediatrician. I've seen a lot of him the past week when I've been walking the floor." He set his briefcase on the counter, dropped his jacket over it and came around to crouch down before the infant seats. He reached out and touched each child, then glanced at her. "Do you think it's okay to have them by the door like this?"

"There's no draft," she pointed out, glad he was willing to drop the reason for her crying spell. "And they're not in direct sunlight."

He nodded and stood up, then nudged the puppy with his toe. The pudgy little animal yawned and rolled over. "What about this little guy?"

"He's spent the day alternately sniffing around the backyard and sleeping. This is about as much energy as he's shown all day."

Will's lips slanted in a smile. "He'll make a good companion for them."

"But not necessarily a good watchdog. I think you should name him Sleepy."

"Sounds appropriate." He glanced around. "Where's Edith?"

Carrie told him, then asked him how his day had gone, grateful that, after his initial comments, he was willing to ignore her dewy eyes and red nose. She prepared glasses of iced tea for the two of them.

It struck her that this was exactly the kind of thing her sister did when Bret came home from the newspaper in the evenings. It was the kind of thing she should have been doing with Robert.

Hard on that thought came the realization that she had to stop thinking in those terms. Will was right. It was time she started climbing out of the well of self-pity she'd dropped into, and the sooner the better. She had to get on with her life.

She told Will that she had called Ginny. "She's going to bring some of my things down this weekend, along with my car. I broke the news about Jacob and Ariana." She glanced at the clock. "That was half an hour ago. I figure by now it's all over Webster."

"Then I can expect calls from my brothers pretty soon. And I'd better phone my mom and sisters in Virginia before somebody else does."

Will made his call, which provoked pretty much the same response Carrie had received from Ginny. Mrs. Calhoun promised to come down as soon as possible to see her newest grandchildren.

After he finished talking to his mother, Will picked up both infant carriers and took them into the living room while Carrie followed with the two glasses. He put the sleeping infants on the floor in front of the sofa and sat down, releasing a long sigh as he did so.

Carrie handed him his glass and jumped right in to what was on her mind. "Will, you said we'd discuss my job this evening."

He lifted an eyebrow at her. "Persistent, aren't you?"

"I have to be. I've got to get on with—with things. Make plans."

"What's the hurry?" He propped his feet on the coffee table and relaxed into the soft leather.

Carrie sat beside him and turned with one knee drawn up. "I quit my job in Greenville because Robert promised I could work with him at the furniture stores, take over the advertising and public relations end of things."

Will lifted a curious brow. "How much was he planning to pay you?"

"We hadn't really discussed that."

"He was probably hoping to get your professional services for free."

Carrie held tightly to her temper. "Believe it or not, Will, I *am* a professional. I wouldn't have let that happen. I know my job and what it's worth."

"Oh, yeah?" Will asked, regarding her with interest. "What's it worth?"

She blinked at him. "Excuse me?"

He waved his glass at her. "Your professional expertise. What does it involve and what's it worth?"

Carrie had to do a quick mental tap dance to switch gears from her growing irritation with him. "Well, um." She stopped and cleared her throat. "I would have been writing up the store's ads for all the local newspapers, promoting specials, getting the store and its employees involved in community activities, things like that—for purposes of public relations."

Will tilted his head and considered her through narrowed eyes. "Sounds like you know what you're talking about—for a woman who really ought to be a writer."

That old argument again. She rolled her eyes and waved her hand dismissively. "Oh, Will..."

He waggled his tea glass at her. "Do you know why I've always thought you should be a writer?"

"No, I don't," she answered sweetly. "But I'm sure you're going to tell me."

He ignored that. "Because it's in your blood. Ginny's a great reporter, so was your dad. Now he's a darned good novelist."

"I know that, Will, but it doesn't mean I'm meant to be a writer, too."

"Bull," Will answered. He took a drink of his iced tea, then sat forward and set it down abruptly. "I need something stronger than this." He stood and stalked into the kitchen. In a few minutes, he was back with a long-neck bottle of beer. After he'd taken a drink, he pointed a finger at her and said, "You're afraid to take chances."

"I got in the car with you yesterday, didn't I?" He scowled. "You know what I mean."

"Yes, Will." She sighed. "You've told me that many times."

"When did I tell you that?"

"On numerous occasions when you were in Columbia on business and stopped to see me."

"Oh, really? Give me an example."

Carrie held up her hand and ticked items off on her fingers as she spoke. "When Dad's first book was published you came up with an idea for a book you thought I should write."

"Oh, yeah," he said, staring into space. "Something about an ax murderer, wasn't it?"

Carrie shuddered. "Uh-huh, and that's not all. Whenever you took me out to eat, if I wanted to order something plain, you wanted me to try something exotic. When we went to the movies, you insisted on seeing psychological thrillers or action pictures instead of—"

"A love story?" he broke in.

"That's right. Love stories are the ones women like." Carrie felt slightly ridiculous pointing it out, because it sounded like she was whining that she'd had no say about where they went on their dates, which hadn't really been dates at all. Certainly they'd never been romantically involved.

Will frowned in annoyance. "Most of those films are sappy. If you'd put your mind to it, you could probably write something better."

Carrie gave an exasperated sigh. "Will, have I mentioned lately that sometimes you remind me of a pit bull disguised in a three-piece suit?"

He frowned thoughtfully and rubbed his chin. "No, you haven't told me that since about a year ago. Round about the time you started dating Robert, the—"

"Don't say it," Carrie insisted, holding up her hand.

"Not over him yet, hm?" Will asked sardonically. "So, did Robert take you to the kind of movies women like to see?"

Carrie tossed her hair and gave Will a defiant look. "Yes, he did."

Will took another swallow of his beer and began moving restlessly around the room. "What else did he do?"

"The kinds of things women like."

"Except show up at the church."

Carrie sat up straight and slammed her glass down on the coffee table, causing both babies to jump. She gave them a concerned look, but they didn't wake up, so she turned her snapping gaze to Will.

Before she could launch a furious attack, he disarmed her by raising both hands and saying, "I'm sorry. That was uncalled for."

"Yes." She blew out a gust of breath that puffed her bangs away from her forehead. "It was."

"Especially since he's out of your life now."

Carrie's stomach clenched at the reminder. "Yes, he is."

Will was quiet for a minute as he considered her. Finally, he said, "Back to my original question. What kinds of things did Robert do that you liked?"

"He didn't argue with me, for one thing," she said wearily.

"Yeah, I figure he was the type to let you have your own way in most things."

"Well, yes, yes, he did."

"Hmph."

Irritated at his tone, Carrie said hotly, "There's nothing wrong with that, Will."

"Hell, no, if a man wants to be a lapdog."

"He wasn't a... Never mind," she said, wrestling with her temper. "Most importantly, Robert knew how to make a woman feel special, how to romance her."

Will dropped into the chair opposite her, set his bottle on the table and leaned forward, hands on his knees. His face looked as though he was ready to burst out laughing. "How to *romance* a woman?"

Oh, lord, Carrie thought. She wished she hadn't said that. Studiously, she examined her fingernails. "That's right," she said in a casual tone.

"This is rich," Will said, barely suppressing the amusement in his voice. "Carrie, I've known many women, dated many. Do you think I don't know anything about romance?"

"How would I know? I never saw that side of you because you were always too busy being bossy and argumentative."

"Oh, really?"

"Yes."

Will looked like he wanted to do exactly as she'd accused him and argue the point further, but he said, "All right, what kinds of things did Robert do to romance you?"

"He sent me flowers frequently."

"I brought you flowers," Will protested.

"Which you swiped out of the flower bed in front of my dorm."

"I only did that once. Besides I was in a hurry," he said, defending himself. Then he hurriedly added, "Tell me more about Robert the Romancer."

A nickname that didn't sound much better than Robert the Wuss, Carrie thought. "He used to tell me things he liked about me, things he appreciated."

"I appreciate you."

"You criticize me," she answered, throwing her hands wide. Restless, she stood and walked over to check on the babies, who were sleeping through the argument. The puppy, who Carrie was more and more thinking of as Sleepy, waddled to his feet, sniffed around the living room a bit, then flopped down to resume his nap.

Will was silent during this interval, but when Carrie straightened and turned around, she discovered that he was standing right behind her. The amusement had faded from his gray eyes, leaving them serious and full of quiet intensity. "There are many things I like about you, Carrie," he said, then nodded toward his children. "Your compassion, for one thing, and your brains, but I've always thought you don't give yourself enough credit for your intelligence."

A lump had formed in her throat. She tried to swallow it. "I don't?"

"Nah. Somehow you think you're in competition with Ginny, but you also think it's really no contest because you think she's smarter than you."

"She is smarter than me—smarter than most anyone I know."

"It's true she has an IQ that's in the stratosphere somewhere, but that's no reason to deny yourself a career as a writer because you think you can't be as good at it as she is."

All of that was true, but no one had ever pointed it out to her before. Naturally, Will was the one to do so. She lifted her chin and cleared her throat. "Yes, well, that's not what we were talking about, is it?"

His eyes searched her closed expression for a second before he said, "No, it isn't. I was taking instructions in romance.'' A smile, slow and sexy, tipped his mouth as he reached up and touched the ends of her chin-length hair. ''I've always thought your hair looked like autumn leaves.''

Stunned, she blinked at him. ''Will?''

''And your eyes, too, though I think they're more of a caramel color.''

''Caramel?''

''And the way you walk. I've always liked how you swing your hips, and that little bounce in your step.''

''You make me sound like a ... bedspring.''

He lifted an eyebrow at her. ''Now who isn't being romantic?'' He frowned. ''Where was I? Oh, yes. What other romantic things did Robert do?''

Carrie almost asked, ''Robert who?'' But she took a step back and cleared her throat. ''He took me dancing.''

''I can dance,'' Will said, affronted.

''The Texas two-step. The shag,'' she scoffed.

''Hey, the shag is South Carolina's official state dance. I like the shag.''

''So do I, but it's not what you'd call romantic.''

''That depends on the person you're doing the shag with.''

Carrie rolled her eyes.

''You want romantic?'' Will's hands shot out. ''I can give you romantic.'' He put his arms around her and pulled her into a slow dance. ''Pretend the Righteous Brothers are on the stereo singing, 'You've Lost That Loving Feeling,''' he ordered.

''Or Michael Bolton singing, 'When a Man Loves a Woman.'''

Surprised into speechlessness, Carrie stumbled along for a few steps, but at last caught his rhythm. They slow-danced their way around the living room. They had never danced before, not even at Bret and Ginny's wedding, but Carrie quickly discovered that he had wonderful rhythm, music or no music.

He ended the dance by grasping her hand, twirling her around once, then placing his arm across her waist and bending her backward until her head was only inches from the floor.

''Will,'' she gasped, scrambling to hang on to his shoulders.

''Relax. This is supposed to be romantic, remember?''

''It would be if all the blood wasn't rushing to my head!''

''I can take care of that.'' Will brought her up a few inches, but only far enough so that he could place his lips close to hers. His breath puffed against her mouth as he said, ''Did Robert end the dance with a kiss?'' he asked.

Carrie's eyes were locked on his. The gray had gone smoky, but she saw his usual stubbornness there. ''Yes, sometimes.''

''Oh. Carrie, you understand that I can't let you think that wuss is more romantic than I am.''

"No, of course not," she breathed. "You have a very competitive nature."

"Just so you understand," he said with satisfaction, and fit his mouth over hers.

# CHAPTER FIVE

IF SHE'D had any breath left he would have stolen it away. His mouth was warm and firm, commanding and yet coaxing her to come along with him as if he had things to teach her—things to learn from her.

Will pulled away and looked at her. "It's even better when you participate," he said, and kissed her again.

She couldn't argue with that. In fact, the only thing she could do was open her lips and give him what he asked for—what she wanted, too, she was discovering.

His arms were wrapped around her. His hands, warm on her flesh, sent tingles through her. After the first few seconds, with her lips following his, she forgot about the argument they'd been having, forgot about Robert, forgot everything, in fact, except Will.

He'd never kissed her before, except for a peck on the cheek, and she was sorry. But maybe it was better that he hadn't. After all, every other man's kiss would have been poor in comparison.

As if echoing her thoughts, Will pulled away again and said, "What do you think? Am I a better kisser than Robert?"

Still too stunned to dissemble, Carrie said, "I...I think you're probably a better kisser than any other man in the United States!"

Satisfaction gleamed in his eyes. "Not in the whole world?"

"I've never traveled outside the U.S.," Carrie wheezed. "So I don't know."

Will chuckled, and the room spun as he stood her upright and held on to her for a moment until her breathing settled down. "You're pretty good yourself, Carrie, and I *have* traveled outside the U.S."

Carrie laughed, pleased that he'd given her ego such a boost. She hadn't realized she had needed it, but it made yesterday's nightmare fade a little more.

Will tilted his head. "You know, I think with a little more practice, I could be as romantic as Robert."

"More so," Carrie croaked, and collapsed on the sofa. She picked up her tea, the ice entirely melted, and took a mighty swallow.

Who would have thought that Will Calhoun could make such an abrupt change?

Carrie touched the back of her hand to her forehead. Whew! When had it become so hot in here? She flapped the neck of her T-shirt, trying to create a breeze on her throat.

"What were we talking about when you started that whole side issue about me being a writer and about Robert being romantic?" she asked when she had her breath back.

Will was grinning at her, but he answered, "Your job."

"Oh, yes, of course. Now, see here, Will. I know I can do the advertising and public relations for your gallery—both your galleries, in fact. We can work it out somehow for me to go to Columbia every week or so, and—"

"You're hired."

"You don't know— What?"

"I said you're hired. I figure you can start out at my galleries on a part-time basis and help out here with Ariana and Jacob, too, at least until I can hire a full-time nanny. As far as salary..." He paused, thinking, then named a figure that nearly had her caramel-colored eyes popping from her head. "How does that sound?"

"Fi-fine," she squeaked, then slumped against the sofa back and fanned herself again. "You don't waste time, do you?"

"No point in it." He drained his beer and set the bottle on the coffee table before giving her a sidelong glance and a grin. "At least once I'd finished stringing you along."

"Brat," she muttered.

"Talk nicely to your boss," he chided. "And there's one more thing."

"What's that?" she asked warily.

"Hold off on getting your own place. I'll be needing you here." His eyes grew dark and unreadable, and his voice dropped to a low tone. "At least at night."

Carrie felt as if a tiny electrical charge had skipped across her shoulders. She shivered, then sat forward, edging away from him. After that crazy impromptu dance, she didn't need this, but she took a quick look at the sleeping babies and said, "Okay. I can stay... for a while, but only until you hire a full-time nanny."

His firm mouth quirked into a grin. "What's the matter? Can't stand my kids?"

"Don't be ridiculous. They're adorable." If he only knew how close she was to falling madly in love with them, he would probably put pressure on her to move right in and stay until they graduated from high school! "I love taking care of them."

"Oh, really?" he asked just as Jacob awoke with a wail. Not to be left out, Ariana joined him. "Time to put actions to words, Miss McCoy. The curtain's going up on the evening colic attack. Take your pick of partners, Miss McCoy. To quote the unforgettable Bette Davis, 'Fasten your seat belts, it's going to be a bumpy night.'"

Carrie smiled at his sardonic comment as she reached for Ariana. Will picked up Jacob. They fed the twins, changed their diapers and began pacing the floor.

At one point, Will said, "Dr. Paul suggests placing them in their bed and letting them cry."

Carrie gave him an appalled look. "At the age of three weeks? What kind of monster is that man, anyway?"

Will shrugged sheepishly and went back to his pacing.

Edith returned from the market and prepared dinner, then headed home to her husband.

Will and Carrie ate in shifts, trading off the babies, who couldn't seem to get comfortable no matter who was holding them or what position they were placed in.

Both of Will's brothers phoned. Carrie heard him tell them to come down on the weekend. At the moment, he couldn't spare the time to talk. They laughed knowingly and hung up.

Will and Carrie continued their floor-walking. Ariana cried softly while Jacob brought down the house, or Jacob quieted for a few minutes only to be disturbed by Ariana's loud wails.

"You'd think the two of them could get this crying thing coordinated," Will said at one point, turning Jacob in his arms so he faced out into the room. "Here, little guy, let's try this position."

Carrie stopped her pacing and gave him a frowning look. "Do you think that's a good idea, Will? It might put too much pressure on his stomach, and he just drank four ounces of formula."

"He'll be all right," Will answered. When Jacob quieted, Will gave Carrie a superior look. The baby promptly spit up on the carpet.

Laughing, Carrie ran for a cleaning rag.

"You're supposed to be the one with the iron stomach," Will complained to his tiny son. "I wonder what Dr. Paul would have to say about this."

"He'd probably say don't press on the tummy of a colicky baby who's just taken four ounces of formula."

Will answered her with a level look, then glanced at the clock and said, "His program is on right now."

"Who? Dr. Paul? Well, by all means turn it on," Carrie said, shifting Ariana from one shoulder to the other. Her back was aching and she desperately wanted to sit down, but whenever she stopped walking, Ariana cried. "Let's see what this paragon of child knowledge has to say."

Will raised a skeptical eyebrow at her, but he switched on the television. Carrie snorted when a wizened little man came on the screen and began talking about toddlers and their self-selected diets.

Carrie thumbed the remote control and switched off the set. "Any more suggestions?"

Will indicated the well-stocked bookcase in the corner of the living room. "He's written a book, too. I just bought it."

Carrie shifted her tiny burden to her left arm and walked over to find the book. She scanned the titles and looked at Will with her eyes wide. "Will, you've got eight books on baby care here."

"Yeah, I figured that if one of them didn't thoroughly cover a certain subject, another one might."

He looked so earnest that Carrie fought down the urge to tease him about his dependence on the advice of so-called experts. "Well, let's see what they have to say."

Gently jostling Ariana up and down, Carrie flipped through each book in turn and closed each in disgust. "Hmph." She snorted. "The majority of these baby doctors say that most babies have colic, there's nothing the parents can do about it, but that everyone survives."

"That's what they think," Will muttered as Jacob pushed the pacifier from his mouth for the hundredth time and began howling once again.

"These people have probably never even seen a baby."

"Then how did they get to be experts?" Will asked.

"They paid somebody to say they were," she answered dryly. "Have you ever actually heard of any of these people?"

"No, but until three weeks ago, I didn't spend a whole lot of time researching baby doctors."

"Believe me, somebody got paid a lot of money to write cover copy that makes them sound like experts."

"Cynic."

She tilted her chin and gave him a direct look. "I'm in advertising, remember? Some people will believe just about anything they see in print."

"Meaning me?" he asked, his gray eyes turning silvery with challenge.

"Meaning you."

"Well, now that you've shot down all my experts, what do you suggest?" Will asked, exasperated.

"What does the twins' pediatrician say about this?"

"Pretty much the same thing these other guys say."

"In that case, I suggest we call a real expert," she said. "Ginny. Brian had such terrible colic that he and Ginny both cried nonstop for the first three months of his life."

She turned Ariana over to Will, and he began strolling the length of the sparsely furnished living room with both babies while she went to the kitchen and called her sister. Five minutes later she was back. When he gave her a curious look, she scooped the children into her arms and said, "You're going to go to the store and buy another rocking chair and two hot water bottles."

"I am?" He pushed his hair off his forehead and gave her a weary look.

"Yes. If you're willing."

"To have a little peace around here, I'd buy every rocking chair in Charleston."

"Then go. I'll hold the fort. When you get back you can tell me what ingenious method you devised to get a rocking chair into a compact convertible."

"That's an easy one," Will muttered as he headed for the garage. "I'll put the top down and place the chair upside down in the backseat. Should be good for a few strange looks on the freeway."

While he was gone, Carrie continued the routine, walking, rocking, patting and soothing, but nothing helped. She was so happy to see Will when he returned that she could have kissed him.

"I've figured out why nature created parents in twos," she said, gratefully turning both children over to him so she could set the new rocker beside the other in the master bedroom, then hurry to fill the hot water bottles. "If one goes crazy during newborn colic, she's got a backup to take over until she regains her senses."

Will didn't answer, and Carrie turned, bright red water bottles in hand, to find him staring at her intently.

"What's wrong?" she asked.

"Every kid deserves a two-parent family, Carrie, but not every kid gets one," he said solemnly.

Her smile faded. "I was joking, Will. I grew up without a mom, remember? Just like you grew up without a dad. I know all about single-parent families." She handed one of the bottles to him and took Jacob in her arms.

He nodded slowly as he looked into her eyes. "Yeah. I guess you do." He paused for a minute, watching her with a serious look on his face. "Of course you do."

Puzzled by his tone, Carrie glanced over her shoulder at him as she led the way down the hall to the bedroom. He followed at his own pace, his speculative gaze on her. She tried to decipher what he was thinking, but it was easier to seat herself in one of the rocking chairs, place Jacob and a blanket on the hot water bottle across her lap and pop a pacifier into his mouth. He quieted immediately. Will did the same, and Ariana quieted, too.

With a grateful sigh, Carrie leaned her head against the chair back and began rocking. After a moment, she laughed softly.

"What's so funny?" Will asked, lifting his head from its resting place.

Carrie's eyes were bright with amusement. "If this is how married couples with newborns spend their evenings, it's no wonder the birthrate in this country is declining."

She'd meant it as a joke, but Will gave her a look that sent prickles of heat running across her skin. "It does throw a wet blanket on a man's romantic notions," he drawled. "I'd say that's probably why nannies are in such demand to help out, especially in the evenings."

Carrie answered with a hollow little laugh. In a heartbeat, the atmosphere had gone from frantic to mundane to intimate. She could hardly keep track of the wild swings of emotions she had experienced in the past three hours—or in the past thirty. She needed to be on her own so she could maintain some kind of balance. As much as she would hate leaving Jacob and Ariana, maybe she should begin looking for her own place, after all.

Five days later, Carrie closed the door on the last departing relative and breathed a sigh of relief. Will's brothers had come down for the day, leaving their children behind but bringing Ginny and Laura. The two women had offered helpful advice and oohed and ahed over the babies, who were exhausted by all the attention and were now asleep.

Ginny and Laura had each insisted they wanted another baby of their own. Their husbands had been equally impressed with Ariana and Jacob, and declared that they would give their immediate attention to granting their wives' wishes.

She turned away from the front door and gave Will a tired smile. "I've never answered so many questions in such a short time in my life. How about you?"

"Why do you think my brothers had me cornered in the den for so long?" Will collapsed on the sofa and stretched his long legs out to rest them on the coffee table. "Sam was offering advice on setting up investment portfolios for the twins, and Bret was taking notes for a newspaper article. He snapped so many pictures my kids will probably have permanent spots before their eyes."

Carrie smiled at his complaint, knowing he was pleased and proud that his brothers and their wives had been so readily accepting of his new family. "Wait till your mother sees them. If her devotion to her other grandchildren is any indication, she'll probably carry a dozen large glossy photographs around in her purse, or maybe a videotape.... What's wrong?"

Will gave her a quirky little smile. "I thought I might stop on my way home from work Monday and buy a video camera."

Laughing, Carrie sat down opposite him. "I think that's a great idea. After all, they grow so fast. Why, they've already grown and changed in the week that I've been here. You really should get everything on tape. They'll want to see it someday.''

Will nodded with satisfaction. ''That's what I thought, too.''

''I can borrow them from you. After I have my own place and don't see them all the time, I'll want to see them on tape.'' Carrie said it lightheartedly, but her throat seemed to close over the words. She was going to hate leaving them after Will found a full-time nanny. In spite of the two a.m. feedings, the evening colic, the moments of frustration when neither she nor Will could decide what was wrong with one or both of them, she had fallen hopelessly in love with Jacob and Ariana.

Just that morning, she had felt an indescribable thrill when Jacob had wrapped his tiny fist around her forefinger and made eye contact with her. Ariana seemed to react to the sound of Carrie's voice. Even when she was hungry, Ariana would frequently stop crying as soon as Carrie spoke to her. She had even smiled at Carrie once, though that was a secret Carrie intended to keep. After all, Will was probably hoping that he would witness all their firsts.

Carrie acknowledged she was beginning to develop a bond with the infants that felt as strong as anything a birth mother could experience. It didn't help that she found it so easy to fall into a partnership with Will. They worked well together in caring for the twins, but she had been careful not to spend the night on his bed again. Instead, she'd insisted he buy electronic baby monitors. She kept one in her room so she could wake when she was needed. Will's eyes had held a teasing light when he'd brought the devices home, but he hadn't commented on her need to keep her distance—which was unusual for him.

Deep in her own thoughts, it was a few minutes before she realized that Will was silent, staring at her in concentration while a frown line stitched itself between his thick brows.

"You'll probably fall in love, get married someday, have a couple of kids of your own and forget all about these two."

"That's hardly likely," she said dryly, then tossed her chestnut hair as she lifted her chin. "Besides, I won't be falling in love again." Even the suggestion filled her with dread.

"Oh? Why's that?"

She wrinkled her nose in a disbelieving grimace. "Because it hurt too much the first time. I don't intend to make that mistake again."

"Not even with someone as romantic as Robert?"

"No. He may have been romantic, but as you've pointed out, he didn't show up at the church. What about you? Will you marry again?"

"I'm not sure yet. Even though it wasn't based on love, my marriage wasn't a mistake." He gave her a lopsided smile. "Look what I got from it."

Carrie's face softened as she thought of the children. "Then it was worth it for you," she said. "It wouldn't be worth it for me."

"I see." He fell into thought again as he studied her in silence, then he roused himself and said, "Are you thinking that no one could take Robert's place in your life?"

Carrie's smile faded. Couldn't he see that the pain was still too fresh for her to discuss this rationally? In fact, she still couldn't discuss it at all without becoming upset, and she hated feeling defensive over it when talking to Will.

She stood abruptly. "No," she said. "No one is going to get the chance to take Robert's place in my life." She turned and left the room. She could feel Will staring after her in brooding silence.

She stopped at a table in the hallway and reached out to touch the blossoms of the yellow roses Will had brought her two days before. She had been stunned but delighted. Their whole silly conversation about his lack of romanticism had produced something good, although she wasn't sure of Will's motives. If she discounted that kiss, she didn't think he was romantically interested in her. She had made it clear she didn't intend to fall in love again, but it didn't hurt to be appreciated.

Strange, she thought. This one gesture from Will meant more than all of Robert's pretty promises and flattery. Maybe because Will was so much busier than Robert had been, and so much more complex. Besides, Robert's defection had thoroughly negated all his romantic gestures.

Carrie didn't want to think about Robert. Ginny had told her he was still making himself scarce around Webster, which just added to the gossip that was circulating through town. Carrie knew she had a starring role in the gossip, too, but she was far enough away that it wouldn't affect her. For that, she had Will to thank.

Over the past week, she'd had time to think about Robert, and she had begun to recall little signs she should have recognized. She saw now that his reluctance to talk should have told her something was wrong.

In the weeks before their wedding day, he had taken several business trips, usually to Atlanta, but he'd never called her when he'd reached his destination. She'd thought it odd, but had been too busy with wedding preparations to pursue the matter. Now she wished she had. She might have some of the answers she needed.

She realized that Robert's parents may have been pushing him into marriage. After all, he was almost thirty and had taken over the family business. They may have pushed him into marriage, thinking it would give him more stability. Poor Robert. She could almost feel sorry for him. Almost.

In her room, she looked around at the suitcases and boxes Ginny and Bret had brought from Webster. She wouldn't unpack everything, only the daily items she needed and the clothes she would wear to begin her new job.

Picking up her largest suitcase, she set it on the bed and flipped it open. Inside, Ginny had carefully packed her best dresses and suits for work. Carrie smiled when she saw that the sleeves of her elegant cream-colored silk dress were stuffed with tissue paper. It was typical of her meticulous sister that she had taken such time with it.

Carrie removed the paper, then held up the dress and shook out some of the wrinkles. She pressed the bodice to her chest and gazed down at the tiny pleats that ran from throat to waist, the delicate buttons, the sweeping skirt that made such a delicious rustle when she walked. She loved this dress, though it was so fancy she'd never worn it. It had been intended for her honeymoon. With a regretful sigh, she tossed the dress over her arm, scooped up an armful of clothes and carried them to the closet.

Once again, she noticed the three cardboard cartons of Lani Gray's belongings. Carrie eyed them thoughtfully as she placed her clothes on hangers and put them neatly away. She had to shift the cartons so her things would hang straight.

For the first time, she noticed that the lid of the top box wasn't sealed with tape as she had thought. She rested her hand on it, thinking about the woman Will had married. What had she worn for her wedding? Probably a hospital gown. What had her thoughts been, knowing that she might not live, might not even see the children she was so determined to bring into the world?

Carrie's fingers slid under the loose flap. What kind of person had Lani been, besides very young and troubled? What kinds of things had been important to a woman who had no family, no real home of her own? What had she left behind to be passed on to the children she hadn't known?

Curious about what was left of Lani's things after the fire in her apartment, Carrie lifted the corner flap she'd been toying with. To her frustration, it was too dark in the closet to see anything, so she tugged the box out a little farther and peered inside. Something soft lay on top. Carrie reached in and drew out an exquisite mohair shawl. Its color was a deep, rich red, and it had long fringe around the edges. With an appreciative little hum of pleasure, she spread the shawl over her hands and examined the basketweave pattern, which was tiny and intricate and made Carrie wonder if Lani had knitted it herself.

She laid it over her arm and ran her hand over the soft wool, thinking that the shawl should be packed away with more care to prevent damage by moths. Ariana might like to have it someday.

"What the hell are you doing?"

With a startled cry, Carrie whipped around to see Will standing in the doorway. His hands rested on each side of the frame, and his thick brows were drawn together in a straight, scowling line. His face made her think of a sea squall approaching across the Atlantic.

"I wish you'd stop doing that. You made me jump out of my skin," she said, gulping for breath.

"I asked you a question." He stalked into the room and came to stand before her.

The grim set of his jaw told her he was truly angry. Eyes full of surprise, she stared at him. Lamely, she waved at the closet. "The boxes were there, and I—"

"Decided to snoop." Will took the shawl from her, folded it and put it into the open carton.

"I wasn't—" she began in automatic self-defense, but he cut her off with a severe look.

Although she didn't quite know why he was so angry, Carrie knew she needed to apologize. She laid her hand on his arm and felt the tense muscles jump beneath her palm. "Will, I'm sorry. I shouldn't have opened that box. You're right. I was snooping because I was curious about what kind of person Lani was, what kinds of things she kept, what kind of mother she would have been to Jacob and Ariana, what she left to them."

"She's dead," he said, lifting her hand from his arm and holding her fingers firmly in his. He looked at them, then into her eyes. The anger was fading, but his gray eyes were dark and troubled. "Does it matter now what kind of person she was?"

"Of course it does. The children will ask about her someday." Carrie gave a little shrug. "I was curious about what kind of answer you'll give."

Carrie found that she was very aware of Will's big, sinewy hand cradling her slim fingers. He must have become aware of it at the same instant, because some intangible force seemed to shift and change in his eyes.

She had never thought of herself as petite, but standing so close to Will, looking into his eyes, she felt small. No, not small, she thought. Overpowered.

She didn't know why she should feel that way. This was Will Calhoun, after all. She'd known him for years, stood up with him at her sister's wedding to his brother, argued with him over her choice of a career—but she'd also danced with him in his living room.

Kissed him.

She told herself that the odd shivers she was feeling were due to his unaccustomed anger, not because she had only recently realized what a truly attractive man he was or because he had rescued her from an embarrassing situation. The strange way she was feeling certainly had nothing to do with the way he woke in the middle of the night, stumbling out of bed, stubble-jawed, sleepy-eyed and sexy as anything, to change diapers and mix formula.

She still found him insufferable at times—whenever he mentioned Robert, for instance.

How on earth had she missed the fact that there was so much raw power beneath his deceptively easygoing exterior? Especially since she was such an expert on how bossy he could be.

His eyes had been full of fire, the anger directed at her, but it had drained away to be replaced by a light that sizzled, sparked, then smoldered.

Carrie blinked at him in wary surprise, wondering where this sudden change had blossomed from. This wasn't the easy relationship they'd shared for the past week. This wasn't even the prickly tension that sometimes sprang up between them. This was that man and woman thing again.

Confused and disturbed by it, Carrie tried to draw her fingers away, but Will's fingers tightened, controlling her backward shift, and pulled her closer.

They had been staring at each other so long and the change in atmosphere had been so rapid that Carrie couldn't remember exactly what she had asked him. Obviously he was more clearheaded than she because he said, "I'll tell my children pretty much what I told you, Carrie—about Lani's background, her talent, how much she wanted her children to be born."

"I—I see." With a nervous little twitch of her eyes, Carrie glanced at the boxes again. "Don't you think they'll need something tangible? Something of their mother's that they can touch and have close to them?"

"Maybe. When the time is right." Will's other hand lifted to cup her shoulder. Its heat and heaviness radiated through her T-shirt. Something about that simple touch told her there was more to this man than she'd suspected, more to this moment than she wanted.

"Carrie, don't you know that in life, timing is everything?"

She licked her lips. "Timing?" What on earth was he talking about? Why was he confusing her like this? Things had been going along just fine. She didn't need these strange feelings that were buffeting her. With a flare of panic in her eyes and a wrench to her shoulder, she broke away and stepped back.

A mocking smile tilted Will's lips. "But time can't be rushed." He crossed his arms and leaned against the closet door. "Do you think you'll be ready to start work on Monday?"

"Work?"

His lips tilted. "Yeah, you know, the type of physical and mental activity for which you receive pay."

She rolled her eyes, glad that they had slipped back to their usual relationship. She could deal with his teasing humor. She couldn't deal with his blatant sexiness. "I know what work is."

"Good." He turned and started for the door. "Then you can come in on Monday and look the gallery over."

"All right." When he started to turn away, she lifted her hand. "Will?"

He paused with his hand on the door frame. "Yes?"

Carrie took a deep breath. This was going to sound silly, she knew it sounded silly, but it was important to her. "I'm going to bring my portfolio," she said, indicating the large zippered leather case propped against the end of the dresser.

"Your portfolio?"

"Yes." She lifted her chin. "I want you to interview me just like you would any other advertising or public-relations candidate."

Will's handsome face creased into a faintly puzzled smile. "Interview you? Why would I do that? I've already told you you've got the job."

"I want to know that I'm getting it on my own merits, for what I can do, and..." Here she faltered.

"And not because I feel sorry for you?"

"That's right." She felt a touch of relief that he understood. "That's exactly right."

"Carrie, I'll look at your portfolio and read your references and then you can show me exactly what it is you can do for my gallery. Believe me, I don't feel sorry for you. I may not agree with your choice of careers, but I respect your abilities."

Carrie felt her temper begin to rise. "If you think I'm in the wrong career, why do you want to hire me?"

Will answered with a soft chuckle as he sketched a wave in the air and turned to stroll from the room. "You figure it out, Carrie."

Carrie made a growling sound deep in her throat and bit her bottom lip in frustration. She would be glad to return to work if only to earn enough money to rent her own place and avoid seeing this disturbing man morning, noon and night.

# CHAPTER SIX

THE Calhoun Gallery was different than Carrie had expected it to be. Given Will's laid-back attitude to most things in life, she'd thought the gallery would have a casual atmosphere—something like a misplaced California beach gallery. While the place didn't have a formal look, it wasn't casual, either.

The building must once have been a home because the sturdy two-story structure looked as if it had been designed with a family in mind. Wide double front doors were flanked by tall, graceful windows and topped by a fanlight, all designed to allow breezes from the Atlantic to sweep in and cool the place in summer. Thick shutters were fastened on each side, ready to be closed in a hurry if those ocean breezes turned into hurricane-force winds.

Carrie paused to look the place over, noting the glistening white paint on the structure, the beautifully lettered sign that proclaimed the building to be the Calhoun Gallery, specializing in American art and featuring work done in the primitive style. Carrie wasn't quite sure what that meant, but it sounded unique and certainly something on which she could capitalize when she got her advertising and public-relations campaign underway.

Before going inside, she turned to survey the neighborhood. Fortunately, Catfish Row wasn't scented with its namesake seafood, which had once been sold from pushcarts along the street. Instead, it was redolent of history and new money. Once a poor section of town, it now sported specialty shops and private homes whose worth she couldn't even guess.

Looking around, Carrie was impressed by the neighborhood, which she had seen only once, years ago, and by the fact that Will Calhoun was successful enough to own a gallery here. Not that she'd had any doubts that he was successful, she thought, turning to the door of the gallery. She just hadn't realized how successful.

Carrie climbed the wide, shallow steps, opened the front door of the gallery and walked into a large room. She looked around, intrigued by the paintings displayed on cream-colored walls and by the waist-high bins of art prints arranged on the floor.

The place was warm and inviting, without the intimidating feel that permeated many upscale galleries. Rooms flowed one into another, connected by wide doorways, inviting patrons to browse.

She wondered if any of Lani Gray's work was on display, but before she could take a good look around, a smiling young woman approached her and said, "Good morning, I'm Brenda Crest. Can I help you?"

"I'm here to see Will Calhoun," Carrie answered with a nervous little smile. "I'm Carrie McCoy."

"Oh, yes. He said you were coming in." She turned and pointed to a staircase that led to the second floor. "His office is right at the top of the stairs. First door on the right."

Carrie thanked her and crossed the room, all the while thinking that this situation was more than a little ridiculous. She had spent the night in his house, shared floor-walking duty with him and eaten breakfast with him less than two hours ago. It seemed silly to have dressed in her best sky-blue suit and sensible black pumps, loaded up her portfolio and driven in to show him what she could offer his gallery when she already knew she had the job. After living in his house for a week and taking care of his children, though, she was determined to show her professional expertise at something other than diaper changing and formula mixing. Besides, Will had his doubts about what she could do to help him out, and she was determined to show him that she could do a good job of promoting and advertising his galleries.

Even as that thought passed through her mind, Carrie frowned, realizing that it wasn't the interview or the job that had been on her mind throughout the ride into town, it was the babies. She knew Jacob and Ariana would be fine with Edith for a couple of hours, and she was silly to worry about them. After all, she wasn't their mother and she was going to be moving out soon. Still, her thoughts were on them.

The top half of the door to Will's office was frosted glass. His name was inscribed in discreet gold letters in the lower right-hand corner, near the knob. She raised her fist and tapped lightly, then paused when she heard him talking on the phone.

"If he won't come to the phone, I'll come to him," Will was saying. "Believe me, this is an offer he doesn't want to miss. Yes, yes, I understand. In about an hour? I'll be there."

When she heard him replace the receiver, Carrie turned the knob and peeked around the door, curious to see Will at work. His office was as neat as she would have expected it to be given what she knew of his personal habits. His desk was an antique rolltop of carefully polished mahogany. The items on top were arranged in precise stacks, one held down by an odd-looking paperweight that seemed to be a hunk of rusted metal.

The desk's little pigeonholes bristled with papers, which seemed to be arranged by color. She would love to know what each color represented.

"Come in, Carrie," Will said, standing and motioning her to a chair positioned beside a high table against the wall.

Carrie sat in the chair he had indicated, an antique ladderback armchair that was surprisingly comfortable. She laid her portfolio on the table, unzipped it and began pulling out samples of her work, press releases she had written and advertising campaigns she had designed or to which she had contributed.

Once she had everything laid out, she began explaining each item. "Many of these ideas can be adapted to suit your galleries," she concluded.

"I need a few minutes to think about these," Will said. "If I have a question, I'll ask."

Carrie wasn't surprised. Will wasn't the type to be rushed into a decision or to let someone else do his thinking for him. She sat back and waited for a few moments, but then, intimidated by his lengthy silence, she stood and began moving around his office.

The walls of the room were painted a restful blue and were crowded with precisely hung paintings and drawings. One especially caught her eye. It was a small painting, no more than twelve inches on each side, and the subject seemed to be a scene of Charleston's famed Rainbow Row, but the houses' vivid light-spectrum colors were muted by clouds gathering in the background and the sight of groups of people, packed bags in hand, walking away from the homes.

Residents fleeing a hurricane, she thought, then read the small brass plaque attached to the base of the frame. *Family Picnic*, it said. Carrie examined the painting again and noted that the bags were actually picnic hampers.

What kind of family did the artist think would set off for a picnic in the teeth of a hurricane? Carrie searched for the artist's name and found it printed in tiny block letters in the lower right-hand corner.

Lani Gray, she read. She rocked back on her heels and gave the work another long look. A family picnicking in a hurricane must represent a family that had been swept away. Carrie recalled that Will had said her family had been lost in a boating accident.

Intrigued but saddened, she turned and found Will watching her. His astute gray eyes took in her distraught face. "See what I mean about her paintings?"

"It makes me feel sorry for her."

"She was a very unhappy person," he agreed, replacing Carrie's work in her portfolio and zipping it shut. "Then when she got pregnant and was abandoned by her sleaze-ball boyfriend and her apartment burned and all the rest of it, well, it was as if all her nightmares were coming true."

"It's so sad. She was so young and never really had a chance." She paused, then said, "Will?"

"What?"

"What are the risks that Jacob and Ariana will develop her diabetes, or her..."

"Depression?"

She nodded, concern filling her eyes.

"I won't kid you, it's high, but their pediatrician says their health depends on their environment as well as their heredity."

"And you're providing a healthy environment."

Will stifled a yawn. "Or I will be as soon as they start sleeping through the night." He stood and flexed his shoulders as if to shrug off unhappy thoughts. He nodded at the portfolio. "Now that I've seen your work, I have a job for you."

She smiled at him. "So you've said."

"I mean today." He glanced at the clock. "In about forty minutes."

Carrie almost protested, but then closed her mouth. She wasn't going to quibble about getting right to work. It was what she wanted, after all. "All right. What do you want me to do?"

"Come along with me as I convince a metal sculptor named Cyrus Little to place his work with us."

Carrie gave him a humorous look. "To watch a master at work?"

"Heck, no," he said, standing and swinging the door open for her. "To show him what hotshot kinds of things we can do for him to make him a rich man."

Will swept her out the door and down the stairs, where he told Brenda where they could be located in case he was needed.

He bundled her into his car and started the engine with the murmured comment that he was going to have to get a car phone.

Carrie smiled. "Was that ever a consideration before you became a father?"

He gave her a sheepish smile. "Nah. I've always thought car phones should be strictly for emergencies—too many people get distracted by them while they drive—and there aren't that many emergencies in my line of work." He shrugged as he pulled out of the parking space and started down the street. "But it's different now. You know what I mean?"

Carrie gave him an ironic look. "I know exactly what you mean. I checked on the twins three times before I left the house and ran back from the garage once to make sure Edith had everything she might need while I'm gone.''

Will's competent hands turned the car smoothly around the corner and he gave her a sidelong glance. ''Why, Carrie, you're beginning to sound like a mother.''

''I know.'' She sighed, and he laughed.

Two hours later, Carrie collapsed laughing onto the front seat of Will's car. ''A woman.'' She snickered. ''A woman named Cyrus. The poor thing.''

Will shook his head in wonderment as he folded himself beneath the steering wheel and started the engine. ''And a man hater, to boot.''

''Can you blame her?'' Carrie asked, her eyes full of amusement. ''Her father named her after himself and spent his life dominating her. Thank goodness she channeled her frustration into her art.''

The woman's sculptures had been unique, and Will was anxious to sign her. She had been highly suspicious of him, however, and would only deal with Carrie.

One corner of Will's mouth crooked up. ''She's quite a character, isn't she? And you handled her like a pro. Seems like you do know your job.''

''That's what I've been trying to tell you,'' she said with a modest smirk.

Will chuckled as he pulled away from Cyrus Little's house. ''I guess this concludes your job interview, Miss McCoy. You're hired. And since we have your employment established, there's one more thing I need your help with.''

"Oh? What's that?"

"Help me choose a nanny for my kids."

For some reason, that made Carrie's heart sink, but she told herself she was being ridiculous. It had been their agreement, after all.

"Sure, Will," she said with a smile that she knew looked sickly. "I'll be happy to, and . . . and maybe I should start looking for an apartment of my own."

He turned to her. "Don't be in too much of a hurry."

"It's time I stood on my own two feet," she said with a firm little nod. "I can't depend on you forever."

Will's eyes narrowed. "Maybe," he said, turning his attention to the road. "Maybe not."

"What was wrong with that one?" Exasperated, Carrie closed the door behind the young woman in the sensible brown dress. Will had frowned all the way through the interview. Carrie had done all the questioning and had been very impressed with the cheerful young woman's credentials. Will's contributions to the conversation had consisted of monosyllables and glances dark enough to suggest that the woman was a potential kidnapper.

Will gave Carrie an irritated look, then reached down to pluck Jacob and Ariana from the new playpen on the living-room floor. He held them protectively against his chest. "I don't think she really likes kids."

Carrie rolled her eyes. "Will, she's a graduate of one of the best nanny schools in this country. She must like kids. Besides, she's the oldest of four herself, so she's been around them a lot, as well."

"Ha!" Will exclaimed, shaking his finger at her. "That just proves my point. With so many kids at home, she probably resents them."

Carrie threw her hands in the air. "That doesn't make sense, Will. You're one of five kids, and you don't resent your brothers and sisters."

"That's different," he said, bouncing the babies gently in his arms.

Carrie walked over and took Ariana from him, straightening the tiny pink elastic hairband she had put around Ariana's dark brown hair, sparse though it was. Ariana's eyes followed the movement of Carrie's fingers, and Carrie smiled at her, hugging her close and kissing her cheek. She took a moment to savor the sweet baby scent of her before she returned to the discussion.

"How is it different?" she asked Will.

"It just is. Maybe because I'm a man."

Carrie raised her head and gaped at him. "Will, I've known you for years and I've never heard you make such a chauvinistic remark before."

He had the grace to look embarrassed for a moment, but came right back. "What about you? That Karen Pearson we interviewed was perfect, but you didn't like her."

Perfect? Carrie thought. Oh, she was perfect, all right. Perfectly stunning, with legs that went on for about six miles, eyes as blue as a Scandinavian fjord and waist-length blond hair. True, the hair had been neatly plaited into a braid and her clothes had been prim enough to gladden the heart of even the strictest of grandmothers, but Carrie hadn't liked the way the woman had looked at Will. Her gaze had latched onto him as if he was the prize bull at the county fair and she was the judge about to pin a blue ribbon on him.

Carrie didn't meet his eyes as she answered. "She was a little too eager for the job. Made me wonder why she'd left her last one."

"The child she was caring for began attending kindergarten at a school with an extended day-care program, so she wasn't needed anymore. Weren't you listening?"

"Of course, I was," Carrie said haughtily. She certainly had been paying attention—in between bouts of ridiculous jealousy over the way Will had been checking out Miss Pearson's quite spectacular legs. Carrie tossed her head in a superior manner. "Besides, she was the only one I found fault with. You found fault with everyone *but* her."

"You're exaggerating."

Carrie knew she wasn't, but she let the argument drop for the moment.

Ariana had wrapped her delicate fingers around Carrie's thumb. Delighted with her, Carrie kissed them and whispered to Ariana how beautiful and perfect she was.

Things had settled down nicely in the past two weeks. Carrie went to work every morning with Will and came home at noon to Jacob and Ariana. So far, Edith had been able to take care of them and keep up the housework, so there was no reason things wouldn't work out well if Will hired a nanny and Carrie moved out.

If they ever found a nanny Will liked.

They'd interviewed six of them in the past two weeks, but none had been up to his exacting standards. In spite of his avowed desire to find a nanny for the babies, Will seemed determined to find someone who was a cross between Mary Poppins, Mother Teresa and Marilyn Monroe.

Carrie gave a little sigh as she admitted to herself that she wasn't sorry the nanny-choosing process was taking so long. The twins were beginning to reach the stage where they stayed awake a little longer each day, so Carrie could play with them. This helped them sleep better at night. Now they usually woke only once for a feeding, then returned to sleep. Carrie and Will could almost sleepwalk their way through the routine of diaper changes, warming bottles and giving feedings.

The two of them would rock the children side by side in the rocking chairs, and every night, Carrie would be very aware of how cozy it was, how right it felt to be there with Will and the twins. They had discovered that the babies were more quiet at night if they were taken out for a walk in the evenings. Will had bought a veritable Rolls-Royce of a baby stroller, a double one, and the two of them took the children for walks on fine evenings. Neighbors were beginning to wave at them and ask after the children as they passed.

People thought she and Will were married and that the babies belonged to them both. It seemed easier not to try to correct the misconception of every neighbor up and down the street. Carrie often fantasized about being their mother and knew it was going to break her heart to leave these babies.

To confuse her even further, Will had taken to heart their discussion about how a man romances a woman. He brought her flowers at least twice a week. They were all over the house. She'd had to go out and buy more vases to accommodate them all. He'd also brought her a small antique chest that had once held exotic teas from China. It was beautifully carved cherrywood. The top was inlaid with a jade design. She couldn't even imagine what it must have cost, but its real value lay in the giver. She was touched by Will's thoughtfulness, but he was making it much harder for her to leave.

"Maybe I was wrong to begin looking for a nanny at all," Will said, breaking into her thoughts. "Maybe that's not what would be best for these two."

Carrie looked up and met his eyes, which were deep gray with his speculative thoughts. "What do you think would be best?"

"A mother."

"That's true." She gave him a puzzled look as she wondered where this was leading.

Will nodded slowly as if all the thoughts he'd been having had come together in one final decision. He walked over and stood before her.

Curiously, Carrie tilted her head.

"In fact, I think that mother should be you."

Carrie gave a start at the way he had echoed her thoughts, and her heart pounded its way up into her throat. "Me?"

"Yes." He reached out and took Ariana from her, then carried both babies to the playpen where he laid them on their backs. Carrie had attached a mobile of circus animals to the railing, and Will gave it a spin before he turned to her.

"Will, how could I be their mother? I'm not . . ."

"You could marry me."

# CHAPTER SEVEN

CARRIE'S mouth dropped open. "Marry you?" Her hand came up to her throat. She could feel her heart pounding against her palm.

One of his straight brows lifted. "Well, you don't have to make it sound like a fate worse than death."

She held out her hands, then dropped them limply to her sides. Her eyes were wide enough to swallow half her face. "It's just that I'm surprised. I didn't know you were thinking of..."

"Marriage," he growled, giving her a sudden, ferocious frown. "You can say it. Surely your experience with Robert the coward hasn't soured you on marriage altogether."

"Yes," she squeaked, breathless because her pounding heart was cutting off her air. "It has I told you how I feel—"

"Yeah, yeah, that no one will take Robert's place. I know that," he said, scowling. "You'll never love anyone else."

Carrie wasn't sure that had been exactly what she had intended to say. "I meant I'm not willing to take that chance again. I admit I love Jacob and Ariana and it...it would be wonderful to be their mother, but..."

"But not if I'm part of the package?"

She threw her hands in the air. "Oh, Will. Don't put words in my mouth. I told you I know I won't be falling in love again."

His brows drew together, and he tilted his head as if he was trying to hear better. "Who said anything about love?"

The heat of embarrassment washed over Carrie. "I just assumed—"

Will cut her off with a slicing gesture. "Don't assume. Carrie, we're both adults here. We both know what we want out of life, and I'm sure you don't have any starry-eyed notions after your experience with Robert, do you?"

Carrie shook her head slowly, then tucked a strand of chestnut hair behind her ear as she gave him an ironic look. "No. I think being jilted at the altar pretty much cured me of starry-eyed notions of any kind."

"Then why not have a marriage that's based on something more substantial?"

Her eyes narrowed suspiciously. "Like what?"

"Mutual interests," he said with a firm nod. "You like working at the gallery, don't you?"

"Yes." Where was this leading? she wondered. "I like it very much."

"You're interested in the artists, the customers, everything about the job. Even better, you're good at it, especially in handling someone like Cyrus Little." He was really warming to his subject now. He began to pace the room from the sofa to the mantel, talking and gesturing. His voice rose and fell as if he was an attorney arguing a case. "You told me you were a professional and knew your job, and you've certainly proved that's true.''

Watching him, Carrie thought this must be the strangest marriage proposal in the history of womanhood. As if to root herself in reality, she looked at the twins. They were completely oblivious to the drama being played out by the adults in their lives and had fallen sound asleep.

Carrie looked at Will, took a deep breath and said, ''I'm glad you appreciate what I'm doing at the gallery, but people don't get married only because they work well together.''

''No, of course not, that's only one reason. We have other things in common, friends, family background, but the two best reasons are asleep right there,'' he said, pointing to the twins.

Carrie glanced at them again, and her face softened. ''It's true that I hate the idea of leaving them, seeing them only on visits or at family get-togethers at Ginny and Bret's.''

''Then don't leave them.'' Will stopped his pacing and came to stand before her. His face was solemn as he reached out and took her hand in his. Her fingers felt icy in his warm grip. ''Carrie, you said that you didn't want to marry again, but I know you want children because of the way you already love these two.''

''I can't deny that,'' she agreed quietly.

''You know what it's like to grow up without a mother, and I know what it's like to grow up without a father. I don't want that for my children. They've already lost their biological mother. They shouldn't lose you, too, just when they're forming an attachment to you.''

He had really hit her where she was the most vulnerable, and she was sure he knew it. The rat.

"Oh, Will," Carrie said, looking at him, her eyes awash in tears. "I...I don't know."

He threw his hands wide. "What can I say to convince you?"

She bit her lip. "You can tell me you're not doing this because you feel sorry for me."

"Sorry for you? Why—"

"Because of what Robert did, because of the way people in Webster are talking." She paused and took a breath. "Because you married Lani out of pity."

"And because she needed my help." Will rubbed his chin thoughtfully. "I can see where your lively imagination would have come up with that conclusion, but this is completely different. Lani was a troubled girl in a desperate, hopeless situation. You're not like that. I happened to come along at the moment you needed help, but even if I hadn't, you would have figured your own way out of it."

"I guess you're right."

"Of course I am. You've always been strong and independent. That's what I've always liked about you."

"I didn't know you liked anything about me."

He gave her a mocking look. "You'd be surprised at the number of things I like about you—or at least I did until you got yourself engaged to—"

"That wuss Robert." She finished for him.

"That altered my opinion of your intelligence somewhat," he admitted. "But you'll redeem yourself in my eyes if you'll marry me."

Carrie couldn't help laughing. "Oh, you're a prince of a fellow."

"Everybody in town thinks so," he said with a grin. "You're the only holdout."

Carrie shook her head at his supreme confidence. "I wish I could be as sure as you are about marriage, but I need time to think."

Will's gaze searched her troubled face. Abruptly, he stepped back, giving her space. "Yes, you do. That's fine. We don't want to rush into anything. You've got to be as sure as I am."

That would be impossible, Carrie thought morosely. As far as she could tell, Will *never* had self-doubts. She was grateful, though, that he wasn't bringing his powerful personality to bear on her. He was giving her time to think rather than keeping up his arguments and persuasions until she gave in.

"All right. I think I'll go for a walk."

"Good idea. I'll ask Edith if she can stay for a while this evening. You and I can go out by ourselves and talk things over."

Carrie nodded and went to her room, where she changed from the dress she'd worn to meet the latest nanny candidate. She put on jeans, T-shirt and sneakers, then picked up the container of pepper mace Will had bought her, insisting that she carry protection since she was now living in the city. She slipped it into her pocket and started for the front door.

Will met her in the hallway. His long, narrow face looked dark and brooding. His ash-blond hair looked as if he had run his hands through it more than once in the past few minutes.

"Carrie?"

"Yes?"

Will moved to stand before her. Reaching out, he took her in his arms. Startled, Carrie stumbled forward, thumping against him.

"There's one more thing," he said, his voice dropping to a low, husky growl. His arms came around her, pulling her tightly against him. One hand reached up to tilt her head to just the right angle, though it was hardly necessary since Carrie was staring into his eyes.

"What?" she wheezed.

"There's this." His mouth lowered to cover hers.

Carrie started to murmur a protest. Except for Will's one explosive kiss the day after she had arrived, it had been years since she had kissed anyone besides Robert. She wondered vaguely why she didn't feel at least a spark of disloyalty to her former fiancé. Instead, she felt a full-blown wildfire of desire for Will. It started as a tiny flame at his first touch and raged stronger and stronger as he prolonged the kiss.

Her senses were immediately filled with Will, the pressure of his firm lips against her soft ones, the intoxicating scent of his skin, the brush of his faintly stubbled cheek against hers—and his taste. Oh, his taste, warm, smoky, delicious.

She hadn't known that fire had a taste.

Releasing her worries, responding to him, Carrie kissed him back wildly and wantonly. Her hands came up to grip handfuls of his gray-striped oxford-cloth shirt, then flattened to feel the pull and tension of his muscles. A deep shudder of need racked his body, but he pulled back and lifted his head.

She pushed herself higher on her toes, hoping to recapture his lips, but he held her away with hands that were just the tiniest bit unsteady.

His eyes were as dark as slate as he said, "Think about that, too, Carrie, while you're deciding whether or not to marry me. Don't think this won't be a real marriage, because it will be. We'll be just as married and just as intimate as any couple who have married for romantic notions. Do you understand?"

Eyes wide, Carrie nodded. In a breathless voice, she said, "You know, that's quite a persuasive technique you've got there."

One corner of his mouth eased up. "Maybe I should have tried it on you more often. I notice it keeps you from arguing."

How would she have any breath left to use for arguing? she thought as she gulped air into her lungs and stumbled down the hall and out the front door. She shut it behind her and filled her lungs with late afternoon air.

Wow. Could that man kiss, or what? Not that she'd had any doubts about it. After all, everything he tried, he did well.

It took her a minute to orient herself, but finally she turned right, following the route she and Will used when taking the twins for a walk.

Head down, hands in her pockets, she sauntered past the home of the Williamsons, an elderly couple who had offered to baby-sit anytime she and Will needed them. What would it be like, Carrie wondered, to be the one to call them up and ask them to baby-sit so she and Will could have an evening out? What would it be like to share equally in all decisions regarding the two little people she'd come to love so much?

What would it be like to be Will Calhoun's wife?

It wasn't as though she would be marrying a stranger, she thought, as she reached the end of the block and turned the corner. She had known Will a long time. They had stood up together at Bret and Ginny's wedding, Will handsome in a tuxedo, she in a midnight blue velvet gown. Even then, she'd thought him appealing, but it hadn't taken her long to realize he was also pushy and opinionated. She had always been intrigued by him, though somewhat in awe and frequently irritated by him.

Carrie reached the small neighborhood park, almost deserted because most of the children had been called home to wash up for supper. She breathed in the honeysuckle-scented air, sat on the deserted merry-go-round and set it in motion by pushing her toes against the edge of the rut worn deep by years of dragging sneakers and sandals.

As she turned in slow circles, her mind returned to her problem. Will was nothing like Robert, who was quiet and steady. She had thought that quietness stood for strength, but now she realized it represented plain old secretiveness.

That was one thing to be said for Will—she would always know where she stood with him, how he felt about things. And she knew for a fact that if he said he'd marry her, he'd darn well show up at the church on the appointed day or die trying.

Abruptly, Carrie stopped the merry-go-round and stood up. She stared at the swing set as if fascinated.

A tingle of awareness ran up her arms. That's what she'd misunderstood about Will all these years, she realized. She'd confused his determination with bullheadedness, and she'd confused Robert's quietness for strength. Actually, it was the other way around. Will was the strong one. Robert's secretiveness had been nothing but a cover for his determination to have his own way.

She wondered if he had ever intended to marry her, or if he'd merely gone along with the plans to hide some purpose of his own—perhaps only to pacify his parents. She didn't know, and the farther he was in her past, the less she cared.

When that knowledge hit her, Carrie felt as if the burden she had been carrying for almost a month fell from her shoulders.

She wasn't in love with Robert. In fact, she wondered if she'd only been in love with the idea of love. She had thought he was steady, caring, genuine, that he had all the qualities she wanted in a husband. It had taken her a month to realize it, but now she knew he'd probably never possessed those qualities.

Will had them. They were at the very core of his character.

Carrie jumped to her feet and hurried from the park along the street toward home. It gave her yet another minor shock to realize that was how she had come to think of the spacious white house with its big rooms and sparse furniture. She and Will could make this house into a real home, one overflowing with the love of two parents for their children.

She hurried in the front door and found Will waiting for her. Her breath caught and her mouth went dry at the sight of him. He'd changed into charcoal-gray slacks and a white shirt whose open neck showed his long, tanned throat. He carried a jacket over his arm.

When she swept in the door, cheeks flushed and hair flying, he gave her a sharp look, then relaxed. "Edith said she can watch the twins. I've made dinner reservations, if you want to change?"

"All...all right," Carrie said, and moved past him into the hall. She wasn't sure what she had planned to say to him on returning to the house, but seeing him waiting for her, looking so masculine, so sure of himself, had scattered her thoughts like leaves before the wind.

Carrie changed into a summery print dress of poppies and sunflowers, buckled on T-strap red sandals and swept her hair into a loosely curled knot on top of her head. She freshened her makeup and sprayed on perfume with a trembling hand, then paused for a moment with her fingers pressed against her jumpy stomach. Maybe going out to dinner wasn't such a good idea. The way she was feeling, she couldn't eat a bite.

Reminding herself not to be a coward, she picked up a light shawl and left her room to join Will. He gave her a swift, encompassing glance, which seemed shaded by approval and said, "All ready? I've put the top up on the car so it won't wreck your hair."

Carrie gave him a nervous smile and licked her lips. "Should we check on the babies before we go?"

He grinned suddenly. "See, you've got a mother's instincts already."

She answered with a quirky little smile as she turned toward his room, where she saw that both babies were asleep in their crib and Edith was sitting in one of the rocking chairs reading a magazine. She gave them a speculative look as she told them everything would be fine and to have fun.

If she only knew! Carrie thought, nerves jumping. One thing this night wouldn't be was fun.

Will held the car door for her, and Carrie seated herself, paying nervous attention to her seat belt, the scenery, the other cars, aware every second of the man beside her. For the past two weeks, every time they'd been alone they'd had plenty to talk about—the twins, the gallery, Cyrus Little and the showing of her work they were planning for the month of August. Now silence stretched between them like an elastic band pulled too tight and on the verge of snapping.

At the restaurant, Will helped her from the car and they walked inside with his hand riding solicitously at the small of her back. They were shown to a booth in a private alcove whose table was topped with a vase of luscious long-stemmed red roses.

Carrie gasped at their beauty. She scooted into the booth and sat staring at them while Will ordered champagne. Finally, she looked at Will.

"Did you order these?"

"Of course." His eyes glittered in amusement. "This place couldn't make a profit if they put a dozen roses on every table."

Carrie cleared her throat. "And you just ordered champagne."

"It's not every night of my life that I get engaged."

She sat back and touched shaky fingers to her forehead. "I haven't said I'd marry you yet, Will."

"Call me an optimist."

"You're an optimist," she said obediently. "And I take back everything I said about you needing to learn how to romance a woman."

"I'm not a romantic."

"Roses, champagne, next you're going to whip out a ring."

Will reached into his pocket and she gulped. "Oh, lord."

He withdrew a black velvet jeweler's box. "Just in case," he said.

"Have you been planning this for a while?" she asked, suspicion ripe in her voice.

"For a while," he admitted. "Did you know I used to belong to Boy Scouts of America?"

"No."

"I still follow the motto Be Prepared."

"I'm sure the Scout leaders would be very proud of you."

Will grinned as he held the box in his fingers and opened the lid. An exquisite pear-shaped ruby in a plain gold setting winked at her from its velvet bed.

"Oh, Will," she breathed. "It's beautiful."

"Does that mean I can put it on you?"

Awash in a confusion of emotions—longing, fear, anticipation—Carrie looked into his eyes. The restaurant's dim lighting didn't lend itself well to reading Will's expression. But she saw a steadiness there that calmed her.

She nodded. "Yes, Will. Put it on me. I'll be happy to marry you."

With a satisfied nod, he took the ring out of the box and held it in his fingers. "I didn't want to give you a diamond because that's what Robert gave you. I want it to be clear from the beginning, though, that there'll be no place in our marriage for Robert."

Carrie looked from the red fire winking in the ring's depths to Will's serious face. "What do you mean?"

"I know you don't love me," he answered bluntly. "But I don't know how you feel about him."

Carrie opened her mouth to tell him what she had realized while she was at the park that afternoon, but he held up his hand.

"I don't want to hear that you're still in love with him, Carrie." His voice had gone harsh, and it was low enough that she had to lean close to hear him. "I don't want to know that."

"All right, Will. I won't say that." How could she, when she knew it wasn't true? She would tell Will that someday, when they'd been married for a while, when she was more sure of how she felt about him.

When he took her hand and slipped the ring on, though, she had to admit that the feelings shivering within her felt very similar to love.

"Are you sure you know what you're doing?" Ginny McCoy Calhoun shoved the front door wide and barreled through as soon as Carrie opened it. Carrie leaped back to avoid being trampled.

Ginny deposited her purse and car keys on the table by the front door and turned to her sister, hands on hips. "Well, answer me. Do you know what you're doing in marrying Will?"

No, Carrie thought, meeting her sister's anxious gaze, but her pride got in the way of truth. "Of course, I do," she said, lifting her chin in a show of bravado.

"Hmph," Ginny snorted. She glanced down, and her eyes widened at the sight of Carrie's engagement ring. "Wow." She choked the word out, lifting her sister's left hand to examine the ruby. "This thing's incredible."

Carrie held it up to the light. "It is beautiful, isn't it?" Since the moment he had given it to her, Carrie had caught herself examining it frequently, turning it this way and that in both natural and artificial lights. Anyone watching might have thought she was being childish, but she felt differently about this ring than she had about the diamond Robert had given her. Its very uniqueness symbolized the difference in the type of marriage she and Will were planning.

"It's beautiful and unusual, exactly what I would have expected from Will," Ginny said, swinging away toward the living room. "Where is he, anyway?"

"At work." Carrie glanced at her watch. "He should be home in about half an hour."

"Good," Ginny said over her shoulder. "That'll give us a little time to talk."

She made a beeline for the playpen, where Jacob and Ariana were lying on their backs, staring wide-eyed at the mobile above their heads. Sleepy had wandered in and taken up his usual napping place nearby.

"Oh, good, they're awake," Ginny said, releasing the side of the playpen and seating herself on the floor so she could pick up and admire first Jacob, then his sister.

"Look how much they've grown in only a couple of weeks," she said, gushing.

"Come right in and make yourself at home, Sis," Carrie murmured, following along in her wake.

"Thanks, I will."

Carrie watched her sister play with the babies and ruefully admitted that she had known this would happen. It was Monday morning. On Sunday night, she had called Ginny to tell her the news of her engagement to Will, then called their father, Hugh. She should have guessed that Ginny would have made the drive all the way across the state in record time to talk about this face-to-face. The only surprise was that Hugh hadn't accompanied her.

Carrie sat on the floor, picked up Jacob and scooted back until her spine rested against the sofa. She lifted her knees and placed him along her thighs. Gently, she swayed him back and forth.

Ginny looked up with a grin. "You're doing a good job with them, little sister," she said approvingly.

Pleased, Carrie said, "Why, thank you, Ginny. It does seem to be getting easier."

"That'll only last until they start to crawl, believe me," Carrie answered with a grin. She smoothed her blond hair from her face. As she studied Carrie's face, the grin faded. "Carrie, I wouldn't presume to tell you what to do with your life."

"Oh, yes, you would," Carrie answered with affection. "You worry over me just like you did when I was little. So does Dad. Where is he, by the way? I would have thought he'd be as hot to get here and talk to me about this as you are."

Ginny shrugged guiltily. "I convinced him to stay home. I wanted to talk to you first."

"Try and talk me out of it, you mean."

"Well, no, not exactly. Not if marrying Will is what you want."

"It is," Carrie said with conviction, but Ginny still frowned. "But you're not sure it's the right thing for me to do."

Ginny shook her head. "No. No, I'm not."

Carrie's certainty faded a bit. It was easy to say to herself that she was sure she was doing the right thing. It was easy to say it out loud to Ginny, but there were still moments when doubts nearly sent her into a panic.

The doubts only came when she thought about her engagement dinner with Will, and his statement that he knew she didn't love him. She knew she no longer loved Robert but wasn't sure exactly what she felt for Will. Attraction, certainly, and respect, but did those equal love?

"Carrie, it's just that the whole Robert fiasco happened less than a month ago."

Surprised, Carrie drew back. "Are you thinking that Will might stand me up at the altar, too?"

"Heavens, no," Ginny said hastily. "He's too responsible for that. Besides, his brothers would hog-tie him and drag him to the altar if he even thought about standing you up."

Carrie smiled slightly. That was true.

"Are you sure you're not marrying Will on the rebound? Just to show yourself and everybody else that you're not such a bad catch, after all?"

# CHAPTER EIGHT

CARRIE'S eyes widened and she blinked. "Honestly, Ginny, that hadn't even occurred to me. Remember, almost everyone in Webster thinks I dumped Robert and ran off with Will. Marrying Will would seem like the next logical step." Carrie lifted her hands in the air and let them drop. "Besides, I've decided I don't care what other people think."

"Fine, then. What do *you* think about marrying Will?"

"I think we'll have a good marriage. We...we certainly know each other well. We have a great deal in common, and we want what's best for the twins." When Ginny responded with nothing but a continued frown, Carrie went on. "You know, in the past few years there have been a number of cases where one biological parent has returned and gained custody of children given up by the other biological parent. Our case is a little different, but if Will and I are married, there would be less chance of Lani's boyfriend coming and taking them—not that it's likely he'd want to," she admitted.

Ginny laid Ariana across her lap and patted her back. The baby's dark eyes stared into the distance as if she was thinking very deep thoughts. "What about love, though, Carrie?"

"Ginny, not every couple is like you and Bret were. You couldn't keep your hands off each other from the moment you met, and you were married two weeks later—"

"And divorced six months later, and married again ten months after that," Ginny finished for her. "Honey, you don't have to tell me that every couple is different. I know that. I also know that even when two people are as much in love as Bret and I, problems still crop up. Sometimes they seem insurmountable. If you don't have love between you, it may seem that there's no reason to keep the marriage going."

"I told you—"

"I know." Ginny held up her hand. "You'll have the kids, but believe me, Carrie, there are times when that will seem like pretty weak glue."

Carrie leaned forward and laid a hand on her sister's arm. "I've thought about all that, really I have, but I think we can make it work. You know how stubborn Will is and how much pride I've got. We'll make this marriage work if only to avoid having you say I told you so."

Ginny smiled, but her eyes were serious as she studied her sister. "I'm really not trying to talk you out of it."

"You don't want me to be hurt. Now, truthfully, do you think Will would do that?"

"No," Ginny admitted sheepishly. Finally, she shrugged and said, "Okay. I've done my sisterly duty, so I'll let it drop now. What kind of wedding do you have planned?"

Carrie breathed an inward sigh of relief that Ginny had moved off the subject. Thoughtfully, she answered, "We haven't talked about it much, but probably a quiet one here at home with only friends and family. I don't think it would be right for us to go to all the preparations and expense that I..." She let her voice die off, knowing that Ginny would understand.

"And what about a honeymoon?"

"We're not planning one." At least they hadn't talked about it.

"Oh, yes, we are," Will said from the doorway.

Both women jumped and whirled around. Carrie watched Will as he sauntered into the room and wondered how long he'd been standing there. For such a big man, he could move like a cat.

He was lazily untying his tie as he came toward them. He pulled it from around his neck and dropped it onto the back of the sofa as he spoke to Carrie. "I made the arrangements today, Carrie. We're going to spend a few days at Myrtle Beach. My mother is coming to take care of Jacob and Ariana."

"Oh, well, that's...that's fine, Will." She wished he had told her sooner. She didn't want Ginny to think the two of them hadn't discussed this, but it was obvious that they hadn't. She gave her sister a quick, sideways glance, but Ginny was watching Will.

He walked over and took Ariana from her, holding her carefully as he said, "Hello, Ginny. Here to talk your sister out of making the same mistake you did—marrying a Calhoun?''

"Let's just say I'm urging caution," Ginny answered in a dry tone.

Will's sharp gaze went from one to the other of them. "Did you succeed?"

Carrie held up her left hand and wiggled her third finger. "I don't jilt. I get jilted, remember?"

"Not anymore," Will said, coming down on the floor beside her. He held his daughter in one arm while he slipped his other one around Carrie's shoulders.

She looked up and said, "That's what I was telling Ginny, and—"

Will cut her off by turning her toward him and closing his mouth over hers. The instant his lips touched hers, the yammering voices of her doubts were cut off as if a door had been slammed on them. His warmth and tenderness filled her, making her lift her chin in welcome. His kiss was long and slow, and when he pulled away, Carrie had trouble even remembering her own name, much less calling up the things that had been worrying her.

"Is it just me, or is it hot in here?" Ginny asked.

Dazed, Carrie glanced over to see that Ginny had pulled her shirt away from her throat and was busy fanning herself.

"It's just you, Ginny," Will answered, his eyes still on Carrie. When she looked at him, he grinned and winked.

Pleasure settled over Carrie like a peaceful shawl. She decided that her doubts were normal, especially given their circumstances. It didn't mean she wasn't doing the right thing in marrying Will.

Will seemed to sense her thoughts. He gave her a smile that was both inviting and provoking because she couldn't tell exactly what he was thinking. It occurred to her that in the next fifty years or so she might spend a great deal of time trying to decipher what he was thinking.

"So, what kind of wedding is this going to be, little sister?" Ginny asked, breaking into her thoughts.

"Hm?" Carrie asked in a distracted tone that gained her one of Will's pirate grins. She sat up suddenly. "Oh, the wedding. We want it simple, don't we, Will?"

"Very simple," he agreed. His arm tightened around her shoulders. "And as soon as possible."

"Simple and soon," Ginny said, tapping her finger against her chin. "I think we can handle that. You're not going to wear your wedding dress?"

Carrie felt Will's arm tighten. She glanced at him and saw that his brows had drawn together, but he didn't say anything.

"No," Carrie answered coolly. "I don't want to wear the dress I bought to marry Robert when I marry Will. Besides, I left my veil hanging in a tree in the woods by the church."

Ginny snorted with laughter. "I wondered what had happened to it."

"I'll wear my cream silk dress, instead."

"Perfect," Ginny said and stood up. "I think I'll go call Laura and see if she has any ideas for this shindig. You know, she used to be in charge of huge events when she worked for the State Department. With her expertise and my ideas, we should be able to do a great job on this wedding.''

When she left the room, Will looked at Carrie. ''Why do I have the same feeling the Yankees must have had when they surrendered Fort Sumter to the Confederates?''

Carrie giggled. ''Because, like it or not, I think we've surrendered control of our wedding to my sister.''

''Oh, well,'' Will said, settling beside her and placing Ariana on his shoulder. ''At least it's all in the family.''

The wedding date was set for the next Saturday at one o'clock in the afternoon. They were to be married in the living room of Will's house. Since there wasn't much in the way of furnishings, they decided it would be easy to move what there was and set up rented chairs.

Will had contacted a local minister, a friend of Reverend Mintnor in Webster. He had agreed to perform the ceremony.

While Carrie and Will were at the gallery on Thursday, Ginny and Laura arrived with masses of flowers to decorate the living room, and a huge grapevine, which they wound around the mantel and stuck full of multicolored silk blossoms. Carrie returned home to find the room being transformed into a fresh and beautiful bower.

When they had finished, Ginny and Laura hurried into the kitchen to discuss the details of the wedding cake with Edith and to explore the possibility of setting up tables and chairs outside for the reception. They were determined to make this small wedding as perfect as possible.

Left alone, Carrie stood beside a tall antique table that Ginny and Laura had filched from Will's gallery. It, too, had been decorated to within an inch of its life and the wedding guest register given a place of honor.

Carrie opened the book and ran her hand over the letters and numbers of her wedding date, which had been embossed on the flyleaf. That was one advantage of having a sister who was highly organized and employed in the newspaper business. She knew where to get something beautifully printed in a hurry.

Smiling, Carrie closed the guest book. She thought it was ironic that a month ago she had been standing beside another guest register for another wedding, and within moments her life had been changed forever.

Certainly it had been changed for the better. She was glad to be marrying Will, to be getting Jacob and Ariana as a ready-made family. Just because her marriage to Will wasn't to be a conventional marriage, didn't mean it wouldn't be a good one.

She heard a step behind her and turned to see Will standing in the doorway holding a large white box. His gaze swept the room and returned to her.

In a stunned voice, he said, "Did my sisters-in-law raid a funeral parlor?"

Carrie approached him with laughter in her eyes. "Try to be tolerant," she advised. "They think they're doing us a big favor."

He glanced around again. "We're going to have to hand out allergy pills to all the guests. We should have eloped."

"They never would have forgiven us. Besides, Ginny and Laura are having fun with this."

Will laid the box on the table beside the guest register. Spying the book, he picked it up and flipped it open to read their names. He gazed at the inscription for several seconds before he took a deep breath, closed the book and replaced it on the table.

Carrie watched him with a puzzled frown. "Will, is something wrong?"

"No," he said quickly, rapping his knuckles on the tabletop as if for luck, then he picked up the box. "Where are the formidable Mrs. Calhouns right now?"

"They dragged Edith outside to discuss having the reception there."

"And the twins?"

"They're asleep."

"Good. Come on in the den. I've got something to show you." He led the way into the room that was very exclusively his, with its collection of wooden bird decoys, antique rolltop desk stuffed with papers and wing chairs upholstered in Black Watch plaid. This was one of Carrie's favorite rooms because it seemed that the essence of Will was embodied here.

Closing the door behind them, he set the box down on his desk and considered her for a long minute before he said, "Carrie, is there any reason in particular that you're not very involved in our wedding plans? That you're letting Ginny and Laura do everything?"

Carrie gave him a dismayed look and leaned against the edge of his desk. Picking up a millefiori paperweight, she passed it from hand to hand.

"I don't know if I can explain this very well," she began hesitantly.

"Try. You're good with words." He sat down in a wing chair and stretched his legs out before him, inviting her, with a wave of his hand, to take the matching chair opposite him.

Carrie shook her head, preferring to remain standing. "When I was going to marry Robert, there was no detail of our wedding that was too small for my attention. I scrutinized and planned absolutely everything. All the parts of the ceremony, the reception, the decorations had to be perfect. Do you know that I even made my bridesmaids try on their dresses and shoes, then I crawled around on my hands and knees and used a ruler to make sure their hems were exactly the same height from the floor? I thought it was vital that they would all look uniform in the photographs."

Will's eyebrow lifted just a bit. "Sounds obsessive."

"It was weird." Carrie put down the paper-weight and rubbed her fingertips against her temples. "I was more focused on the wedding than on the relationship and the man I was marrying."

"And you think that was why Robert jilted you?"

"I don't know." She shrugged. "Maybe, but I'm not going to make that mistake again. This time, I'm trying to keep in mind that the marriage is more important than the ceremony."

Will propped his elbows on the arms of his chair and steepled his fingertips together. Looking at her over their tips, he said, "Come here."

Cautiously, Carried walked over to him. He reached up and snagged her wrist, pulling her onto his lap.

With a squeak of surprise, she fell across his thighs. "Will, what are you doing?"

He wiggled his eyebrows at her. "Working on the marriage by practicing for the honeymoon."

Carrie pressed her palms against his chest and leaned away from him. "I wonder how many girls in this world have fallen for that ploy."

"I don't know how successful other guys are with it, but you're the first one I've tried it on. Let me know how it works." He brought his hands up between hers and snapped them out so that she fell against his chest. With a soft chuckle, he folded her into his arms and kissed her.

By the time Carrie recovered her senses, she was drowning in him. His warmth and tenderness swept through her, filling her with needs and desires. She put her arms around him and returned his kisses.

After a few minutes, he drew away. "How'm I doing?"

Carrie ran her tongue over her swollen lips and said, "Could be better. Practice makes perfect, you know."

Will laughed, kissed her again, then held her with one arm while he stretched the other one to snag the white box off the desk. He dropped it onto her lap. "Wedding present for you," he said.

"You're kidding. You've already bought me a dozen things."

"This is special. Open it."

Obediently, Carrie removed the top and folded back layers of shimmering silver tissue paper to reveal a negligee of midnight blue silk. Her breath catching in her throat, Carrie lifted it out. "Oh, Will," she whispered. "It's beautiful."

The gown was cut low in front and even lower in back with thin spaghetti straps to go over the shoulders. The matching robe had long, loose sleeves and lapels embroidered in white satin floss.

"This is so you'll know this isn't going to be a marriage in name only."

"I didn't think it was." Carrie folded the garments into the box and set it on the floor.

"I'm not going to be your buddy." Will's voice had gone low and fierce. "We're not having a platonic relationship of any kind. I wasted five damned years like that."

"I'm not sure what you mean, Will."

He cut her off by kissing her again, and by the time he was finished, she'd forgotten her question.

Will set her on her feet, then stood beside her, supporting her while she tried to get her lungs working again. She was puzzling over the question she had meant to ask him when the phone rang.

She cleared her throat. "I think Edith's outside with Ginny and Laura. I'd better answer that." She stumbled slightly as she moved toward the desk.

Grinning, Will stepped back so she could pick up the phone from the desk, then walked to the doorway, where he leaned against the doorjamb and watched her with his eyes dark and smoky.

Shivering at the look in his eyes, Carrie picked up the receiver. "Hello?"

Silence greeted her, then a hesitant voice said, "Hello, Carrie? This is Robert."

Carrie felt all the color drain from her face, then rush back again. "Robert." She croaked the word out, her eyes automatically snapping to Will, who had sprung away from the door. "Why are you calling me?"

"I know you're staying with Will Calhoun. Marcia said that you're working for him now, but I was wondering if we could meet somewhere."

"Meet somewhere?" She was finally regaining her equilibrium. "You mean now?"

"Yes. I drove to Charleston today, hoping that I could see you."

"Are you kidding?"

"I know I don't have any right to ask, after what I did, but I owe you an apology, and, well, I'd like to explain."

Will crossed the room in two steps and put his hand over the mouthpiece. "Tell him you can't talk to him." His face was as fierce as his tone of voice.

Taken aback by Will's demand and flustered by Robert's shouts for attention, she jerked the receiver out of Will's grasp, told Robert to wait a minute and covered the mouthpiece with her hand.

"Why can't I talk to him, Will? Because you say I can't?"

"Damned right," Will snapped. "You're going to marry me in two days. You have no reason to talk to him."

"No reason?" She waved the receiver at him. "I'd like to know why he dumped me!"

"It doesn't matter now. You're going to marry me. He's out of your life. He doesn't matter."

Carrie stared at him for several seconds—at the harsh line around his mouth and the level determination in his eyes.

She couldn't remember a time when he had ever looked this formidable. In spite of her shock over Robert's call, she realized this was vitally important to Will.

She had been raised to be strong and independent, to know her own mind and make her own decisions—to be in charge.

Looking into Will's eyes, though, she realized that this was one time she would have to surrender—or at least compromise. And wasn't that what marriage was? A series of compromises? As much as she wanted to know Robert's reason for jilting her, her greater concern was for Will.

Her eyes on Will's, she moved her hand from the mouthpiece and said, "Robert, you and I don't have anything to say to each other."

Over his squawking protest, she rattled the receiver onto its hook. She realized her hands were shaking badly, so she pressed them against her stomach.

Will reached out and lifted her chin. Placing a light kiss on her trembling lips, he said, "You're going to marry me in two days. Robert Gallatin had his chance, and he blew it. He has no place in your life—in our lives."

He stepped back, then turned and left the room, closing the door behind him.

Will's reaction was what had her sagging against the corner of the desk for support. She'd never seen possessiveness like she'd just witnessed in his eyes. It surprised her, but it also gave rise to soaring hope.

She knew he desired her. He'd never kept that a secret, but this was something more, something that made her heart pound and her palms sweat.

She was afraid to give it a name because that meant she'd have to face the fact that her reasons for marrying Will—his reasons for marrying her—weren't as clear-cut and simple as she had thought.

The next two days passed in a blur for Carrie. Will had made reservations for all their family members at nearby motels so they didn't have to deal with the responsibility of taking care of guests. Carrie had offered to move to a motel until after the wedding, making way for more family members, but Will wouldn't hear of it, pointing out that it would soon be her house, too. Besides, it might upset the twins' routine, which she didn't want to do.

Sam and Bret arrived along with their children, and both families were in and out of the house frequently, helping Carrie get things ready. Although she enjoyed the controlled chaos of their presence, Carrie soon discovered that two tiny babies were just too enticing for three preschoolers who thought they could be played with like living dolls.

The day before the wedding, Carrie found three-year-old Brian trying to lift Jacob to a window so he could see the cars on the street outside. She rescued Jacob and took him and Ariana into Will's room, where the three of them could lie down on the bed and try to recover from the attentions of their family members.

During this respite, Carrie had only to look at the two babies to know she was doing the right thing. She could see how much they had grown since she had come to stay. Their faces were fuller, their color was good, their dispositions pleasant—except when they were in the midst of one of their continuing bouts of colic, but even those seemed to be decreasing.

She turned on her side and put her arm around the two tiny bodies, snuggling them close. Whatever was good about these two, she had added to it. As their mother, she could continue to do so for the rest of their lives.

She stayed on the bed with them, talking and urging them to focus their eyes by holding up a squeeze toy shaped like a hippopotamus. They didn't exhibit much interest and after a few minutes they dozed off.

When the door opened and Will walked in, she looked up and smiled. "Hello."

Except for two o'clock feedings, they hadn't been alone since Robert's phone call. Carrie examined Will's face for remnants of yesterday's disagreement but saw his usual easygoing smile.

Hands on hips, he stood and looked at her for a few seconds. His eyes swept over her, taking in her bare legs beneath the hem of her denim shorts and her loose T-shirt, which had ridden up above the waistband and showed a slice of skin. Warmth sifted through her, pooling in her stomach as she met his eyes.

She was glad that he liked what he saw. She certainly liked what she saw when she looked at him. She liked him best when he didn't look too perfect, and that's the way he looked right now. His hair was ruffled, and she knew that had probably happened when he had picked up Nancy for a kiss. Their niece liked to leave her mark on anyone she hugged.

Will's tie was already unknotted, and the ends dangled down his chest. Carrie didn't know why he even bothered to wear one, he seemed to hate them so.

His lips tilted in a lopsided grin. He jerked his thumb toward the living room. "My brothers, my two sisters-in-law and my adorable niece and nephews are out there laying waste to my house, and you're in here lying down on the job," he teased. "You ought to be ashamed."

Carrie rolled to her back and propped her head on her hand. "Oh, I am. I am," she assured him, grinning. "Just as soon as I finish lazing around here, I plan to rush right out there and help them in their destruction."

"You don't seem to have much respect for my property."

"No, I don't."

Will took a pen and a small notebook from his shirt pocket and wrote something down.

"What are you doing?"

"Making a note to put this house in your name as soon as we get back from Myrtle Beach."

"Will! You can't do that!"

He tossed the notebook onto the dresser top where it came to rest beside a box of disposable baby wipes. "It's my house. I can do whatever I want with it."

Her eyes wide, she said, "But what if our marriage breaks up? I'll have the house and you won't have—"

"Our marriage isn't going to break up," he answered firmly. "I thought you understood that." He came to the bed and tapped her hip, urging her to scoot over so he could sit down. When she complied, he settled beside her and said, "I haven't worked for this for so many years to have it break up. If we have any problems, we'll work them out."

Carrie frowned at him. "What do you mean you've worked for this?"

"I mean I've been planning marriage for a long time," he said smoothly. "But it's not something I enter into lightly. When I married Lani, I knew it wouldn't last because I knew she was dying." Being careful not to disturb the babies, he placed his hand on the pillow beside Carrie's head and leaned over her. "Make no mistake, Carrie Diane McCoy, this marriage will be permanent."

Carrie licked her lips. "I see."

"You didn't expect us to have a prenuptial agreement, did you? Believe me, it wouldn't be necessary because it would never be used. For as long as I live, I'll be your only husband."

"You're very sure of yourself." Carrie couldn't control the tiny quaver in her voice.

"And I want you to be, too."

Carrie looked into his solemn eyes and read the promise there. Tentatively at first, and then more boldly, she reached up and grasped the ends of his tie. She exerted steady pressure until he came down to her level. "If I wasn't sure of you, Will, I wouldn't be here." She lifted her chin and kissed him.

# CHAPTER NINE

WILL seemed startled for an instant—after all, she'd never initiated any kind of intimacy between them before—but he quickly slipped his arms around her and kissed her back. Every time she kissed him, Carrie felt herself open more fully to him. The more he held her and kissed her, the better she knew him, and after what happened when Robert had called, she wanted to show him how she felt. At last, she pulled away and said, "Just so we understand each other."

His eyes were deep gray and calm. "Oh, I understand."

Carrie cleared her throat and responded in a breathless tone. "So it's safe for me to assume that you won't leave me at the altar?"

Will stood up. "That's right. Since the altar's going to be right in my living room, I don't think it's likely I'll forget to show up." He grabbed her hands, pulled her to her feet and gave her another quick kiss. "I don't plan to be a fool like Robert Gallatin."

It was in that instant that Carrie realized she truly loved him. He was everything she wanted in a husband, in a man. She loved him, but she didn't quite know how he felt about her and she didn't know how to tell him. Would he even believe her?

After all, she'd thought herself in love with Robert only a month ago. Shaken, she leaned her head weakly against his chest.

His arms immediately came around to cradle her. Misinterpreting her sudden weakness, he said, "Carrie, you don't have to worry. Everything's going to be fine."

She tilted her head and looked into his eyes, though she could hardly focus on him for the tears that were suddenly swimming in her own. "I know that, Will."

He frowned slightly and looked as if he wanted to say more but she stepped away and took a couple of quick swipes to clear away the tears. His hands fell to his sides where he opened and closed them into fists a couple of times.

At last, he moved around her and picked up both babies. He handed Jacob to her and said, "My mother and sisters just called from their motel. They're on their way over to meet these two. Do you think you're ready for more Calhouns?"

"Why not?" she asked, laying Jacob down once again for a quick diaper change. "I've met them before, I like them, and I'm going to be one of them."

"Oh, no!" Will said, pausing with his hand on the doorknob.

"What?"

"I just realized, now that I'm adding you and Ariana to the family, the Calhoun women are going to outnumber the Calhoun men."

Carrie grinned. "Who says there's no justice in this world?"

Will gave her a retiring look as he opened the door and ushered his little family out.

"Carrie, are you ready?"

Hands held against her fluttering stomach, Carrie turned to her sister and said, "As ready as I'll ever be," then winced as she realized she sounded like she was embarking on something she didn't want to do, which wasn't true at all.

"I'll tell Bret to start the music, then." Ginny hurried out. Within moments, Carrie heard the beginning notes of Handel's *Water Music* coming from the stereo in the living room.

Carrie nervously gave herself another examination in the mirror. The dress was beautiful, but she feared it made her look too pale. She grabbed a makeup brush from her traveling case and added blush to her cheeks. Satisfied, she nodded. She just wished it was as easy to remedy the wild apprehension in her eyes and the butterflies in her stomach. Since realizing she was in love with Will, Carrie had become even more worried about their marriage. It had been easy to say she was marrying him for the sake of the twins, but now she had to admit she was marrying him for her own sake. She wished she knew how he really felt.

A swift rap on the door announced her father. Without waiting for an answer, Hugh stalked in. He was a small-framed man with graying hair and the assertive nature of an old-time newspaperman.

"It's time, honey, unless you want to call the whole thing off."

Laughing, she walked over and took his arm. "Not a chance. I thought you liked Will."

"I do, but I don't want to see you hurt."

"Will won't hurt me," she assured him as she gave him a hug. "Everything's going to be fine." She smiled, knowing that her assurance came from her certainty of Will's faithfulness.

"Well, all I've got to say is that I'm glad I don't have any more daughters for these Calhouns to marry," he grumbled.

Laughing, she straightened his tie and kissed his cheek. "Dad, you know you like Bret and Will. You always have."

"Maybe so, but I think I'd like a little more variety in my sons-in-law." Hugh brightened suddenly. "On the other hand, this one does come equipped with a couple of grandkids for me."

"There you go," Carrie said, tucking her hand into the bend of his elbow where he patted it possessively. "What more could a father ask for?"

"For you to be happy."

"I will be, Dad," she assured him. She picked up her bouquet of pink roses and lavender and said, "Let's go."

He gave her a searching look, and seemingly satisfied, walked out the door with her and down the hall to the living room. As they approached, Ginny signaled Bret and the music changed to the wedding march.

When they stopped in the living room doorway, Carrie's gaze scanned the room and fastened on Will, who stood with the minister before the flower-bedecked fireplace.

Will was dressed in a beautifully tailored gray suit that gave him an air of solemn distinction. When he saw her, his eyes brightened as if he was happy to see her after a long wait. He lifted his hand as if to draw her forward.

Seeing him, knowing how she loved him and trusted him, Carrie felt the nervousness that had plagued her all day give way to calm certainty. Smiling, she tightened her hand on Hugh's arm and walked forward to marry Will Calhoun.

"Does your dad always cry like that?" Will asked three hours later as they set off for their honeymoon.

Carrie laughed as she waved to the crowd of relatives standing on the sidewalk. They were busy throwing rice, birdseed and flower petals at Will's departing car.

Will's mother lifted Jacob and one sister held Ariana up to see their parents drive away. Carrie was glad the babies would be cared for by their grandmother and aunts, but she knew she would still worry about them.

When they turned the corner and the house disappeared from sight, she settled into her seat and answered Will's question. "No, I've never seen Dad cry like that. Does he know something about you I don't know?"

Will lifted an eyebrow at her. "He probably knows a great many things about me that you don't know, but maybe he got so emotional because you're his baby."

"Perhaps, although he did tell me he's glad I'm married."

"And he said to me he's relieved he doesn't have any more daughters who can be spirited away by the nefarious Calhouns."

"He told me that, too, but he didn't use the word nefarious."

"He's a writer," Will pointed out. "He likes to use big words." He gave her a sideways glance as he turned onto the street that would take them onto Highway 17 leading to the Grand Strand and Myrtle Beach. "So how does Miss McCoy feel about marrying a Calhoun?"

"Happy," Carrie admitted. She looked at the diamond-encrusted wedding band that encircled her finger along with the ruby engagement ring. The set was breathtaking, and looking at it made her feel well and truly married.

There hadn't been time to write their own vows, as she and Robert had done, so the minister had used the traditional wedding ceremony. Carrie found it fitting, but somehow ironic, since theirs wasn't starting out as a traditional marriage.

Will seemed satisfied with her answer. He gave an approving nod.

As he drove up the coast, he told her about his plans to buy her a new car, one with a high safety rating and built-in infant seats for Jacob and Ariana.

Carrie agreed that such a car was a necessity, but when he began describing all the features and options he wanted, she sighed.

"What's wrong?"

"You're so practical, Will. I feel like the honeymoon is over before it's even begun."

He gave her a swift look. "More of that talk about me not being romantic, hm?"

"I did think you were making real progress in that area."

"Until now?"

"Until now."

"Looks like I'll have to do something to change your mind, Mrs. Calhoun," he answered.

"Looks like you will." Carrie gave him a quick grin, then turned to sit facing forward and watch the passing scenery. Her smile faded as into her mind sifted the memory of what he had said the night he had proposed—that she shouldn't confuse romance with love.

For a minute she felt sad, but she found comfort when she began mentally counting off all she was gaining from this marriage.

When they reached the hotel, Carrie's jaw sagged. The entrance to the multistoried building was elegant with red-jacketed car attendants ready to park the Mustang. The place was surrounded by acres of golf courses and gardens, making it look like a white jewel placed in a velvet setting.

"What do you think?" he asked when the bell-hops had taken their luggage and the attendant had driven the car away. "Will this do?"

"It's wonderful, Will. Beautiful."

"Better than the place Robert was going to take you?"

Carrie had to smile. Will was the most self-possessed man she knew, but he still seemed to resent Robert.

"I don't know, Will. I never made it to the place on Hilton Head, remember?"

"And I'm damned glad."

Will took Carrie's arm, and they entered a lobby filled with flowering plants and ferns that swayed in the air-conditioning. There, they registered for the first time as husband and wife.

Even though it was the height of the summer tourist season, Will had managed to book a suite for them. When the bellhop opened the door, Will swept her into his arms.

"Will, what are you doing?" she cried, scrambling to hold on to his shoulders.

"You're a smart woman, I can't believe you don't know I'm carrying you over the threshold." He set her in the middle of the floor, admonished her not to move and tipped the grinning bellhop. When the young man had left, Will went on. "Tell me the truth, on a scale of one to ten, where would you rate that as a romantic gesture?"

Laughing, Carrie tossed her purse onto a settee and said, "It was about a seven."

Will's face fell. "Only a seven? I'll have to do better than that." He threw his hands wide. "How about this room?"

Carrie looked around. The suite had a breathtaking view of the surf, which was visible through big glass doors. The furnishings were wicker and rattan, with print cushions in bright primary colors, which gave the place a South Sea Islands feel. She saw champagne chilling in a bucket of ice. On the table beside it were two glasses and a vase of red roses, at least two dozen.

From where she stood, Carrie could see that the color scheme was carried through to the bedroom, which had a king-size bed exactly like the one Will used at home—which they would both use when they returned, and not in the platonic way they had on her first night in his house. More roses, combined with forget-me-nots and lavender, were in a vase on the nightstand. Fat white candles shared space with them.

At the sight of the bed, the roses, the candles, Carrie's mouth went dry and she turned away.

Will, of course, had seen where she had been looking, but he didn't comment.

"I would say this place is a solid...eight," she declared.

"What would a ten be?" he asked.

"A room overlooking the French Riviera," she responded promptly.

"Keep dreaming, wife, keep dreaming."

She snickered, but her humor died away when Will started walking toward her. He slipped his arms around her. "Let's see how you would rate our first kiss as husband and wife."

She tilted her head and looked into his eyes. "We've already had our first kiss as husband and wife."

"That was for public viewing. This is strictly private." Will lowered his head and captured her lips with his own.

She had kissed him so many times, Carrie thought hazily, but each time had been different, and none of them had ever been like this.

Maybe it was the feel of his arms around her, tight and strong. Maybe it was the way his lips parted hers forcefully. Maybe it was the way his hands ran over her back, then up to cup the back of her head, or the way he held her just so as his mouth devoured hers. Perhaps it was the low, throaty sounds that came from deep in his chest.

This kiss was different because it was strictly possessive.

His scent and taste went through Carrie's head in a rush of heat as his mouth touched, tasted, explored. The longer he prolonged the kiss, the more Carrie's heart hammered in her chest until she was sure he must feel it through the silk of her dress and the broadcloth of his shirt.

When he pulled away, she noticed his breathing was as ragged as hers. "Well?" he asked, his eyes hot and wild.

"Tha—that was definitely a ten," she gasped, lifting her hand to press it against her heart.

"Good. I'll try to maintain that rating for the rest of our married life."

"I don't doubt that you'll succeed."

Chuckling, Will brushed his lips over hers. "Are you hungry?"

Desire sizzled through her. "That depends on what you mean by hungry."

"For food. We have dinner reservations at eight."

Carrie lifted her arm and glanced at her watch. "It's only six now."

"That means we have two hours to kill. We could go for a walk on the beach."

She reached up and began loosening his tie. "We could."

His eyes narrowed, but she could see the heat building once again in them. "We could order something to drink and sit out on the balcony."

"Sit and chat. That's a good suggestion." She tossed his tie aside and started unbuttoning his shirt. "But we've already got champagne."

Will's arms shot out and he dragged her close. "Oh, the hell with it," he said in a husky voice.

He picked her up once again and carried her into the bedroom. On her scale of romantic gestures, Carrie knew that rated a ten. When he set her down beside the bed and began unbuttoning the pearl buttons that ran the length of her cream silk dress, Carrie forgot all about the silly rating system and concentrated on the moment.

Will lowered his head and kissed each inch of skin he bared. "Carrie," he murmured against her throat. "I don't want more children yet."

She felt as if her skin was melting beneath his touch. She was too busy feeling to concentrate on his words. "What?"

"Did you prepare for this? Are you using birth control."

She shivered. Why did he have to get so practical all of a sudden, she wondered, but she answered. "Robert insisted that I start taking birth control pills." She felt the sudden tension in Will's hands, but she finished, "I stopped taking them, but started again when you asked me to marry you."

"Good. That'll make things easier."

He crushed her mouth beneath his in a way that was just short of violent. His hands grasped her waist, then her bottom, pushing her against him. Startled by the strength of his arousal, Carrie murmured a protest and tried to pull away, but he held her tightly.

Dizzily, Carrie tried to keep pace with the change in him. He had been so tender, but now it was as if he was trying to stamp her with his possession.

What had she done? Said? Then she recalled the mention of Robert. She knew that in Will's mind, Robert was a fool, but even the mention of his name seemed to have the power to disturb Will—which shouldn't surprise her when she recalled the way he had reacted when she had talked to Robert on the phone.

She managed to wedge her arm between them and look into his glittering eyes. "Will," she gasped through swollen lips. "Don't you understand? I started taking the pill in preparation for marriage."

"Yeah. I got that part." His nostrils flared as he fought to control his breathing.

Touched by the strength of his passion and at how hard he was trying to keep his jealousy from lashing out, she said, "Will, I never slept with Robert."

His eyes widened, then narrowed until he was looking at her with a ferocious scowl. "What?"

"I wanted to wait, and he didn't push the issue," she said with a hollow laugh. "Of course, I know now it was because he didn't really love or desire me."

Will's face cleared, and a smile began to spread slowly over his face. "Well, thank God for that," he murmured, then stepped back abruptly. "Keep my place," he said. "I'll be right back."

While she stared at him, he called the front desk and told them to cancel the dinner reservations. He picked up a book of matches and lit the candles beside the bed. A faint vanilla fragrance soon began drifting through the room. Next, he flipped the Do Not Disturb sign above the knob of the outer door, grabbed the champagne and glasses, opened the bottle, poured them each a glass and handed her one.

"How'm I doing on the romantic scale?"

Carrie swallowed her heart, which had jumped into her throat. For some reason, her eyes were brimming with tears. "You're racking up perfect tens," she said, choking.

"Good," he answered, satisfaction ripe in his voice. "Now, how about a romantic toast?"

"I'm listening."

Will looked into her eyes. His own were dark gray with his thoughts. "To Carrie Calhoun," he finally said. "This will be her only wedding night."

As Carrie clinked her glass against his and drank, she reflected that it was a very strange toast and certainly wasn't very romantic. To her, the most romantic toast would have been one that ended with him saying I love you, but she knew that wasn't going to happen.

The heady rush of champagne filled her head, and she said, "This is decadent."

"No, it isn't," Will answered, taking her glass from her and setting it down along with his own. "Give me about five minutes, and I'll show you real decadence."

Then his mouth was on hers, greedy and giving. His hands skimmed over her, opening enough of her buttons that he could wrest the dress from her shoulders, down her arms, off her hips until it lay crushed on the floor. Her underthings followed, then his clothes, too. With an impatient growl, he kicked them all aside and turned down the bed with a jerk of his wrist.

Then they were on the bed, his hands, her hands, everywhere, their mouths seeking, touching, fulfilling.

Longing and need shuddered through her, but no sooner had she experienced them than Will satisfied them. His hands skimmed over her, touching and then kissing the points of her collarbone, her breastbone, her breasts.

Her hands kneaded his back, then his arms, touching at last those muscles she had admired and finding them as hard as she had suspected they would be.

He pressed her into the bed, and she welcomed him into her body because he already filled her heart. As he took her to heights of sensual pleasure, her heart cried out what her lips couldn't speak—her love for him.

She felt colors and lights spinning through her mind until the pleasure burst over her in a shower of golden sparks.

For several minutes afterward, neither of them spoke. In fact, neither of them seemed able to breathe. Finally, Will lifted his head and said, "Are you okay?"

"Wonderful," she answered in a breathy voice. "I can honestly say that I've never felt better."

He chuckled and moved to cradle her against his side. Carrie reached over and ran her nails through the sandy gold hairs that furred his chest.

"There were times when I thought this day would never come," he said lazily.

Carrie raised herself on her elbow and said, "You mean your wedding day?"

His glance sliced to her. "Yeah, I mean my wedding day." He lifted his head and pressed his mouth to her throat, murmuring something that sounded like, "To you," but Carrie couldn't be sure because he was doing delicious things to her and leading her back the way they had just come.

*     *     *

By midnight they were famished. Instead of calling for room service, they dressed in jeans and T-shirts and hurried out to the parking lot, where a grinning attendant muttered something to Will as he turned the Mustang over to them. Once they had started off in search of some fast food, Carrie turned to her new husband, who was grinning smugly.

"What did you say to that guy?"

"What guy?"

"Don't be dense. The parking lot attendant, of course."

Will stopped for a red light and gave her a sheepish sideways glance. "Uh, nothing."

"Will..."

"Married less than twelve hours and already a nagging wife," Will said in a self-pitying tone.

"Will!"

"Oh, all right. He said, 'Congratulations, buddy.' "

"Congratulations for what?"

"For getting married, I guess."

Carrie rolled her eyes. "Oh, come on. How could he possibly have known we were newlyweds?"

The light turned green, but Will took a second to reach over and flip open the lighted mirror on her sun visor. As he accelerated, he said, "Look at yourself."

Obediently, Carrie did so, and gasped. Her hair was mussed, her eyes bright, her lips swollen and her lipstick smeared. "You did that on purpose," she accused.

"What?"

"Just before we left our room, you grabbed me and kissed me so I'd look like a—"

"A newlywed?" Will supplied. "A happy bride? Yup, I sure did."

Carrie's momentary pique evaporated, and she dissolved into giggles. That's exactly what she was.

Will pulled into an all-night convenience store. He stopped the car and turned to her. "Can't blame a guy for wanting to let other men know you're off-limits."

Will helped her from the car, and they went inside. As they chose snacks and soft drinks and set them on the counter before a sleepy-eyed clerk, Carrie thought about what he'd said. Will wanted people to know she was off-limits to other men, that the two of them belonged together. A thrill of happiness swept through her. It wasn't a declaration of undying love, but it was certainly a solid message of commitment.

As Will reached for his wallet, she linked her arm with his and smiled at him.

She wasn't going to ask for more than that right now.

They stayed in Myrtle Beach for a week, swimming in the ocean and in the hotel pools, playing tennis, walking on the beach, dining out in the fabulous seafood restaurants that made the area famous and shopping. Carrie bought so many outfits and toys for Jacob and Ariana, Will swore his credit cards were going to experience a meltdown from overuse.

They ventured down the coast to Georgetown, once an important port serving the rice plantations that thrived in the area. They visited Brookgreen Gardens to admire the sculptures and Ripley's Believe It Or Not Museum to gawk at the oddities.

Mostly, though, they stayed in their suite and made love. Will was a tender and considerate lover, and Carrie was glad that she had waited for him. She fell more in love with him every day and thrilled to hear him say that he loved the way she made him feel, the way she touched him, the way she looked, especially in a bikini—which he wouldn't let her wear outside their suite, and which ended up as two bright orange scraps of fabric on the carpet.

Carrie reveled in him and in their time alone together. In spite of the unconventional reason for their marriage and Will's insistence that she not confuse romance with love, Carrie was sure he would come to love her as she loved him. She wasn't worried. They had plenty of time—the rest of their lives, in fact.

# CHAPTER TEN

WILL and Carrie fell into a surprisingly congenial life together. For two weeks after their return from their honeymoon, they spent almost all their time together, either at work or at home caring for the twins. Will contacted his attorney, who began making arrangements for Carrie to adopt Jacob and Ariana.

Carrie continued to work half days while Edith cared for the children. By the time she arrived home in the afternoons, both babies were awake, and she delighted in their time together.

At almost three months, their evening colic attacks were becoming less frequent, and they had begun to make eye contact with their parents, smile and make babbling sounds. Will was firmly convinced that they were geniuses and would begin speaking in complete sentences any day now.

Between the satisfaction of caring for the babies and the undivided attentions of her sensual husband, Carrie was awed by the complete happiness of her life. She fell more in love with Will every day and couldn't imagine how or why she'd been so reluctant to love him sooner. In some ways, she was eager to tell him how she felt, to know how he felt about her, but she was reluctant, fearing he

172

would say it was too soon for her to know her own feelings.

One day, Carrie took one of their artists to lunch to discuss an upcoming showing of the woman's work and the promotional activities Carrie intended to do beforehand. Will promised to join them if he could get away.

After their meeting, the artist departed and Carrie began gathering her things and placing them in her portfolio when someone approached her table. Thinking it was the waiter, she glanced up to ask for her bill, but was shocked to see Robert Gallatin.

"Robert!" she said, with a jolt. "What are you doing here?"

"You wouldn't talk to me on the phone, you wouldn't meet me, so I came to Charleston and followed you from Calhoun's gallery."

"Robert, I don't like the idea of you following me, and I really don't think we need to talk."

"Carrie, please. I've been wanting to talk to you for weeks. You have to give me credit for that much—and I did wait until that other lady was gone. We both need a better ending to... to our engagement. You deserve better than what I did."

Even Will wouldn't argue with that point, Carrie thought. At last, she said, "All right, Robert. Sit down."

Uncertainly, Carrie watched him slide into the booth across from her. This whole idea made her distinctly uncomfortable, but she was curious about what he would have to say. Even though she knew she hadn't loved him as much as she'd tried to convince herself she did, she truly felt regret over the way things had ended between them.

As he sat, Carrie tried to view him dispassionately as she would a total stranger.

She was surprised to find that it didn't hurt to see him, as she had thought it would. Instead, she discovered that, after the first rush of discomfort, she didn't feel much of anything beyond curiosity about why he wanted to see her.

She found it odd that, without her view of him colored by love, he was really quite ordinary.

Unlike Will, Robert was not a big man. Her eyes were on an equal level with his. His build was compact, his hands and feet small.

"Thanks for... for listening to me, Carrie." He made an awkward little gesture. "Would you like anything else to eat? Or a drink, maybe? A martini, wine?"

Carrie gave him an appalled look. In her opinion, it was far too early for anything alcoholic, and she intended to keep a clear head. "Nothing, Robert."

With a distressed shift of his eyes, Robert nodded, placed his own order for a martini with a passing waiter and then said, "Carrie, you're looking good, really good."

"I'm not exactly pining away," she answered.

"That's good, that's good. I didn't want you to pine away," he said in a falsely hearty tone. "But I was surprised when I heard that you'd left the church with Will Calhoun."

Carrie raised an eyebrow at him. "There was no reason for me to hang around."

"No, uh, no, of course not."

The waiter returned with the martini. Robert, who Carrie knew wasn't much of a drinker, swallowed nearly half of it in one gulp. He ordered another, and she finally got fed up.

"Robert, why don't you just tell me why you jilted me, why you want to see me now, and then we can both go home."

He winced at her blunt tone, but he finally said, "Well, all right." He took a breath, pausing long enough to make her want to thump him on the head, but he finally said, "I guess you noticed that I wasn't quite myself for the last few weeks before..."

"The wedding," she prompted. Good grief, why was he having so much trouble saying what was on his mind?

"Yes, that's right. Anyway, I'd been getting a lot of pressure from my mom and dad to get married."

"I sensed that," she admitted.

"They were going to sign the business over to me completely if only I'd get married."

"That's why you proposed to me?"

He took a swallow of his fresh drink. "Partly. Well, mostly."

Carrie rested her forehead on her fingertips. "I thought you loved me."

"I thought I did, too. Carrie, I didn't mean to hurt you, but a few weeks before the wedding, I was on a trip to Atlanta."

"I remember."

"I met a girl there."

Carrie looked up. "You met a girl?"

"She's a dancer."

"A dancer?"

"Yeah, you know. A bunch of us got together, furniture retailers, designers. We were at a convention and we all went to this club together. She was onstage," he said in a tone that reeked of nostalgia. His eyes had a faraway look. "She had on...well, never mind what she had on, but from the first minute, it was magic."

Carrie's jaw dropped. "Magic? You're telling me that you dumped me for a dancer in a girlie show and it was...magic?"

Robert realized he'd said the wrong thing and immediately tried to mop up. "Not that I didn't love you in my own way."

Carrie didn't think her ego could take much more of this. "And what way was that, Robert? You just said your parents were pushing you to marry and you met another girl and that's why you dumped me. Do I just about have the facts straight?"

Robert finished his drink and signaled for a third. "Yeah, that about covers it, except that, well, things happened between us that night, and she, uh, she got pregnant."

Carrie stared at him for a full minute, trying to take this in. "And you knew this before our wedding, didn't you?"

He couldn't quite meet her eyes, but he said, "Yeah."

"Why on earth didn't you tell me then? Why did you let me go ahead with all the plans and preparations?"

"I was embarrassed, okay?"

"Well, I should think so!"

"Everything was moving so fast. It was like...like being on a runaway train. I couldn't think of any way to stop it, to get out of the wedding."

"Except to send poor Marcia with that cowardly little note. I can't believe this." Carrie shook her head. "I absolutely can't believe this."

Robert didn't answer because he was busy finishing his third martini.

"You know something, Robert? I always respected you. I thought you were truly a gentleman. I thought all those romantic things you did, the flowers, the moonlight walks, were really important, but Will's right. You're a coward."

Robert looked ready to wilt. "I know you're disappointed in me, and I deserve it."

Seeing him like this, Carrie felt sorry for him, and all her anger drained away. "Oh, Robert. I never thought you were the type of person who wouldn't face up to your responsibilities."

"I'm going to. I'm on my way to Atlanta tomorrow to marry her."

Wearily, Carrie reached for her purse and jacket. "I hope the two of you will be very happy. What's her name, by the way?"

Robert gave her a sappy grin. "Boom Boom LaFlame."

It was too much for Carrie. She stared at him for several seconds before she broke into peals of laughter. "Boom Boom LaFlame? You're marrying a woman named *Boom Boom LaFlame*?"

Robert's grin faded into surliness. "Hey, you don't have to say it like that. She's a nice girl."

Carrie laughed again. Her mind had manufactured a picture of Boom Boom in a skimpy sequined costume drinking tea with Robert's refined mother.

"Oh, oh, yes," Carrie gasped. "I'll just bet she is nice. I'm sure she'll get along well with the other ladies in Webster. Maybe she can give dance lessons to the Library Guild and the Ladies' Club."

Robert drew himself up. "Carrie, that's very uncharitable of you."

Yes, it was, but Carrie couldn't help it. Holding her sides, she collapsed against the back of the booth and hooted with laughter. All around them, people turned to stare.

Robert glanced around furtively, then reached over and grabbed her shoulder. "Cut it out," he growled. The liquor he had consumed was beginning to hit him, turning his surliness into nastiness. His grip tightened on her shoulder.

"Ouch, Robert, stop that!"

"Take your hand off my wife before I break it."

"Oh," Carrie gasped, whipping around to see Will Calhoun bearing down on them. "Will, I didn't know you—"

"Would follow you?" he asked silkily. "Obviously not, Carrie."

Robert wobbled to his feet. "See here, Calhoun, you have no right to be so heavy-handed."

Will stopped before them, reached down and pulled Carrie to her feet. "Seems to me that you're the one being heavy-handed, Robert, and with my wife, too."

The second time Will used that word, Robert finally caught on. "Your wife?"

"That's right." Will lifted Carrie's left hand to show off her rings. "We've been married for three weeks."

Robert's eyes narrowed. "Was this going on while you were engaged to me, Carrie?"

Carrie gasped in outrage, but Will cut her off. "Don't you think, after what you've done, that you're the last person to be asking that question?"

"Well, I don't know about that," Robert blustered. Although he listed somewhat when he stood, he tried to face down Will. Even sober he couldn't have done it. Intoxicated, he was no match at all.

With a hollow little laugh, he looked at Carrie. "I've explained everything now, Carrie, so I'll be going. I hope you'll be very happy."

"The same for you and—" Carrie paused, knowing that she would break out laughing again if she said the woman's name. "Anyway, have a happy life."

Robert put some money on the table, turned and walked carefully away. Outside, he hailed a cab and disappeared.

"Whew," Carrie said. "At least he didn't try to drive."

"Probably the only wise thing he's done today," Will growled as he picked up her portfolio, took her arm and propelled her to the front counter. He paid Carrie's lunch check in stony silence and hurried her toward the door.

Carrie gave him a cautious look. "Something wrong, Will?"

"Oh, no," he said as he stiff-armed the door open. "I just love tracking you down and finding you in a tussle with another man—your former fiancé."

"I wasn't in a tussle with him," Carrie defended herself, but he wasn't listening.

"Why did you meet him, Carrie?"

"I didn't meet him."

He gave her a furious look.

"You know what I mean. I met him, but I didn't instigate the meeting, if that's what you're asking."

"It is," he said. Outside the restaurant, he stopped beneath a magnolia tree, dropped her portfolio against its base and turned her to face him. "Explain."

Carrie felt her temper elevating by quick degrees, but she answered, "He came to Charleston today purposely to see me and followed me here from the gallery. When I was alone, he approached me and said he wanted to explain what happened, why he'd stood me up."

"And so you trotted right off to meet him?" Will's gray eyes were flinty, his jaw like marble.

"I didn't trot off anywhere. I told you, he found me." Carrie tossed her head. "You must know I've wondered why he jilted me."

"He did it because he's a coward."

There were a number of reasons, but she would tell him about them later, when she wasn't so irritated with him.

With her jacket in one hand and her purse in the other, she defiantly crossed her arms over her chest. "Will, I'm glad I talked to him. I needed to."

Will's lips drew together. Moving forward, he crowded her against the trunk of the magnolia. Fallen white blossoms were crushed beneath their feet, but Will paid them no mind. "I told you, there's be no place in our marriage for Robert Gallatin."

"I'm beginning to think there won't be room in our marriage for the two of us and your stubbornness," she replied angrily.

"Thinking of backing out, Carrie? It's too late for that."

"No. I'm thinking you need to listen to me when I try to tell you something or we're not going to have much of a marriage."

Will's eyes lit with challenge as he leaned closer. "And what is it I'm supposed to be listening to? Your excuses for your old fiancé?"

"I'm not going to make excuses for him."

"Did he even bother to tell you the truth? Did he mention a certain dancer named Boom Boom LaFlame?"

"Yes, he told me all... You *knew*?" Horrified, she stared at him.

Will's jaw tightened as if he wished he could call back his words. "Yes, I knew," he answered slowly, then finished in a rush. "I had a private detective check up on him, found out he'd met this girl and that she said she was pregnant. I had the detective's report with me. I was coming to your wedding early so I could show it to you, but I found you on the road instead, and..."

"And I just went right along with you." Carrie vaguely recalled a blue file folder Will had moved to the backseat, then hidden in a drawer, then finally stuffed into his briefcase and taken to work with him.

"Yes, and thank God you did!"

Carrie shook her head as she stared into his face. Weakly, she leaned against the magnolia. "You knew," she said in a hurt tone. "You knew and you didn't tell me?"

"I didn't hire the detective until a few days before the wedding, after Ginny told me Robert had taken to disappearing—"

"Ginny knew, too?"

"No, no. Stop interrupting, damn it!"

She lifted her chin and glared at him.

He released an exasperated breath. "I didn't want to call and tell you what I'd learned. It wasn't the type of thing that anyone should hear over the phone, and I was busy with Jacob and Ariana."

"What made you think you had to be the one to check up on Robert? Who appointed you as my—"

"Because I've been in love with you since you were eighteen years old!" Furious, he turned and paced away from her, then swung back, his face holding a look of profound shock. He took a breath, held it for a second, then said, "Did I just say with I think I said?"

Carrie stared at him, then nodded slowly as the truth seeped through her. "Yes. You . . . you said you've been in love with me since I was eighteen. Why didn't you tell me before?"

Will's fists clenched at his sides. "Because you were too young. I was older, already in business. I was determined to have you, to make you love me, to marry you, but I came on too strong and scared you off, threw you right into Robert's arms."

Carrie's hand lifted to where her heart was pounding in her chest. "Will," she said faintly. "Will, you should have told me. I never knew. I thought you saw me as some kind of little sister or someone who needed to be guided and advised."

"I know. I know." Will shrugged. "I messed it up all the way around. I wanted to woo you, but I was so afraid you wouldn't love me that I pushed you and bullied you and made Robert look even more attractive."

Unable to speak, Carrie lifted her hand.

Will gave her a cautious look, but he came to her and took her hand. "It happened at Bret and Ginny's wedding. I'd seen you before, of course, but I thought you were a kid, then you came down the aisle ahead of the bride in that midnight blue dress and I was a goner. I've always been a sucker for that shade of blue on a beautiful woman."

Carrie smiled, thinking of the negligee he'd bought her. "I must have been very self-centered, because I didn't have a clue."

"I hid it from you, tried to just be a friend, but I had to see you, be near you. That's why I opened the gallery in Columbia long before I planned to. It gave me a reason to come and see you while you were in college. I thought after you got used to me, I could make my move, but instead, I blew it. You got the job in Greenville, then started dating Robert. I saw my future slipping away, and there was no one to blame but myself. I didn't want to marry anyone else, but Lani needed me, the babies needed me. I could have the family I wanted even if I couldn't have you."

"You overwhelmed me," Carrie admitted. "I had to work very hard not to fall in love with you."

Will drew her into his arms. "And now?"

"Now I love you very much." Joy bubbled up, filling her eyes with tears. "I thought I would be overtaken by your strength and determination. Somehow I never understood you would use it only to protect me." She gave a shaky laugh. "In fact, I didn't know that until you asked me to marry you. I love you, Will. Thank you for not giving up, for pursuing me."

Will kissed her. "Believe me, Mrs. Calhoun, the pleasure is all mine."

She wrapped her arms around him and held on tightly as she kissed him. She remembered, now, all the hints he had given her in the past few weeks, hints of how he really felt, of how long he'd waited for her, how much he wanted her. She had been incredibly dense not to have figured it out before.

Finally, she pulled away and gave him a dreamy smile. "Why don't we go home and see our kids?"

"Sounds like a better idea than standing here and shocking the passersby," Will agreed. "Then maybe we can send Edith home, put the babies down for a nap and have some time alone."

Carrie gave him a flirtatious look. "Would this time alone happen to involve a certain midnight-blue negligee?"

His eyes twinkled at her. "Yep."

Carrie sighed and kissed him again. "I love a man with a one-track mind. Let's go home, husband."

"I hear a baby." Will mumbled sleepily into his pillow.

"Must be one of ours," Carrie answered, snuggling up to his side and pulling his arm around her.

He placed a kiss in her hair and said, "We've only got one, remember? The other two are four years old, which they tell to everyone they meet."

"At this point, we should just be grateful they've made it this far. Who would have thought that two kids who had such a shaky start in life would turn out to be so rambunctious?" Carrie put a hand down to stop Will's wandering hand, which was furtively making its way up her thigh. "On second thought, they are a great deal like their father."

Will laughed and turned her onto her back so he could do a more thorough job of kissing her, though he was careful of her sensitive breasts. He was really giving the kiss his best effort when a small, indignant voice piped up from the doorway.

"Mommy, Daddy, Jake says I can't carry Anna Lee because I'm too little." A small figure clothed in footed pajamas hurtled across the room and bounced onto the bed.

Groaning, Will rolled over and sat up, carefully pulling Carrie up with him.

"It's not true, is it, Daddy?" Ariana coaxed. Her bottom lip stuck out, and her black hair was a tangle around her head, making her look like a petulant Gypsy. Carrie smiled fondly at her as the tiny girl continued. "I'm not too little. I'm 'xactly the same size as Jake. He's just a billy."

"Billy?" Will mouthed the word to Carrie, who shrugged.

"I think she means bully." She gave Ariana a hug and a kiss. "No, you're not too small. You're just perfect, and you're a big help with the baby."

"I knew it," Ariana said with a nod. "But you're going to have to tell Jake that."

"Absolutely," Carrie agreed.

Will started to rise from the bed, but he sank down again when Jacob entered, proudly bearing his downy-haired four-month-old baby sister, who greeted the world with wide blue eyes and a sunny smile.

Jacob laid the baby down on the bed, then handed his father a diaper. "She's poopy and she's hungry," he announced. "And I'm not fixing her."

"Thanks, son," Will answered. "We'll take it from here."

"Edith's here," Jacob said. "She's gonna make pancakes."

With a whoop, Ariana scooted off the bed, and the two children dashed for the kitchen.

With another laugh, Will took the gurgling baby into the bathroom to change her diaper while Carrie sat up and prepared to nurse their daughter. She smiled as she thought about how complete her life was. Jacob and Ariana were wonderful children, and she loved them as much as she loved Anna Lee. Their biological father had never shown the slightest interest in them, so her adoption of them had gone through without a hitch. The things that had belonged to their birth mother were carefully packed away, waiting for the day when they would be told about Lani, and about how much she had loved and valued them. Will had been right when he'd said they needed a two-parent family. It took the energy of both of them to keep up with Jacob and Ariana.

Carrie smiled, Will had been right about something else, too. She hadn't told him yet, but a few months before Anna Lee's birth, she'd begun writing a children's story. After talking to one of the gallery's artists about doing the illustrations, she had written up a proposal for the book and mailed it off to a publisher, who seemed interested.

She would tell Will all about it when it was an accomplished fact. No point in giving him an opportunity to say I told you so.

When Will came back, he handed Anna Lee over, then arranged pillows behind Carrie's back and beneath her arm so she would be comfortable. Then he climbed into bed and put his arm around his wife and daughter.

Carrie kissed Anna Lee's soft head, then grinned at her husband. "On a chaotic morning like this, do you ever regret picking me up on the highway that morning?"

"Uh-uh. Do you ever regret getting in the car with me?"

"Not for a moment. I realize now that a marriage with Robert never would have lasted."

"Nah, in the marriage game, he's a real loser. Even old Boom Boom didn't stick around very long, did she?"

"No."

"I would love to have seen the look on Robert's face when she told him she wasn't really pregnant, then filed for divorce a month after the wedding." Will shook his head. "She sure took him to the cleaners," he added in a tone of deep satisfaction.

"Marcia tells me that he rarely even dates anymore. Since Boom Boom, he's really had to buckle down and pay attention to the family business. He almost lost it in the divorce settlement. I feel sorry for him."

"Don't," Will said, leaning in to give her a long, slow kiss. "Concentrate on your family. On me."

"I do." She smiled, kissing him back. "In fact, when I'm through feeding this baby, I'm going to take her in to Edith and you're going to get my undivided attention."

Will treated her to a smoldering look. "Mrs. Calhoun, I'm all yours."

She reached up and pulled his head down so that her lips brushed his. "Forever," she agreed.

# Harlequin Romance ®

brings you

SIMPLY THE BEST

## Authors you'll treasure, books you'll want to keep!

Harlequin Romance books just keep getting better and better…and we're delighted to welcome you to our Simply the Best showcase for 1997.

Each month for a whole year we'll be highlighting a particular author—one we know you're going to love!

Watch for:

**#3445 *MARRY ME***
by Heather Allison

TV presenter Alicia Hartson is a romantic: she believes in Cupid, champagne and roses, and Mr. Right. Tony Domenico is not Mr. Right! He's cynical, demanding and unromantic. Where Alicia sees happy endings, her boss sees ratings. But they do say that opposites attract, and it is Valentine's Day!

Available in February wherever Harlequin books are sold.

# Take 4 bestselling love stories FREE

## Plus get a FREE surprise gift!

---

## Special Limited-time Offer

**Mail to Harlequin Reader Service®**

**3010 Walden Avenue**
**P.O. Box 1867**
**Buffalo, N.Y. 14240-1867**

**YES!** Please send me 4 free Harlequin Romance® novels and my free surprise gift. Then send me 6 brand-new novels every month, which I will receive months before they appear in bookstores. Bill me at the low price of $2.67 each plus 25¢ delivery and applicable sales tax if any*. That's the complete price and a savings of over 10% off the cover prices—quite a bargain! I understand that accepting the books and gift places mo under no obligation ever to buy any books. I can always return a shipment and cancel at any time. Even if I never buy another book from Harlequin, the 4 free books and the surprise gift are mine to keep forever.

116 BPA A3UK

| | | |
|---|---|---|
| Name | (PLEASE PRINT) | |
| Address | | Apt. No. |
| City | State | Zip |

This offer is limited to one order per household and not valid to present Harlequin Romance® subscribers. *Terms and prices are subject to change without notice. Sales tax applicable in N.Y.

UROM-696  ©1990 Harlequin Enterprises Limited

# You're About to Become a *Privileged Woman*

Reap the rewards of fabulous free gifts and benefits with proofs-of-purchase from Harlequin and Silhouette books

# Pages & Privileges™

It's our way of thanking you for buying our books at your favorite retail stores.

PROOF OF PURCHASE

HR-PP21

Offer expires March 31, 1997

### Harlequin and Silhouette— the most privileged readers in the world!

For more information about Harlequin and Silhouette's PAGES & PRIVILEGES program call the Pages & Privileges Benefits Desk: 1-503-794-2499

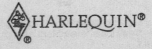

HARLEQUIN®